It would be a hell of a lot easier to psych himself into confronting an armed perp than to face delivering a baby....

Armed with a plastic drop cloth and a stack of worn-but-clean towels, Dan went back and prepared the couch the way Fay had told him to.

"Thanks," she said. "If I hadn't seen your light..." Her words trailed off and she began to take deep breaths.

"Another contraction?"

She nodded, and he knelt beside her, tentatively resting his hand on her abdomen. Through the flannel cloth, it felt rigid as a board. He checked the second hand of his watch. Before he could move his hand, something thrust against it, surprising him. Damned if the baby hadn't kicked him. The realization made him smile. Feisty little thing. Dan decided the most reassuring thing he could do for Fay was to keep his mouth shut about how inexperienced he really was. Strange how people assumed cops delivered lots of babies.

"Um, Dan? It's coming—"

And without hesitation, he sprang into action....

Dear Reader,

Well, if it's true that March comes in like a lion and goes out like a lamb, you're going to need some fabulous romantic reads to get you through the remaining cold winter nights. Might we suggest starting with a new miniseries by bestselling author Sherryl Woods? In *Isn't It Rich?*, the first of three books in Ms. Wood's new MILLION DOLLAR DESTINIES series, we meet Richard Carlton, one of three brothers given untold wealth from his aunt Destiny. But in pushing him toward beautiful—if klutzy—PR executive Melanie Hart, Aunt Destiny provides him with riches that even money can't buy!

In *Bluegrass Baby* by Judy Duarte, the next installment in our MERLYN COUNTY MIDWIVES miniseries, a handsome but commitment-shy pediatrician shares a night of passion with a down-to-earth midwife. But what will he do when he learns there might be a baby on the way? Karen Rose Smith continues the LOGAN'S LEGACY miniseries with *Take a Chance on Me*, in which a sexy, single CEO finds the twin sister he never knew he had—and in the process is reunited with the only woman he ever loved. In *Where You Least Expect It* by Tori Carrington, a fugitive accused of a crime he didn't commit decides to put down roots and dare to dream of the love, life and family he thought he'd never have. Arlene James wraps up her miniseries THE RICHEST GALS IN TEXAS with *Tycoon Meets Texan!* in which a handsome billionaire who can have any woman he wants sets his sights on a beautiful Texas heiress. She clearly doesn't need his money, so *whatever* can she want with him? And when a police officer opens his door to a nine-months-pregnant stranger in the middle of a blizzard, he finds himself called on to provide both personal and professional services, in *Detective Daddy* by Jane Toombs.

So bundle up, and take heart—spring is coming! And so are six more sensational stories about love, life and family, coming next month from Silhouette Special Edition!

All the best,

Gail Chasan
Senior Editor

Please address questions and book requests to:
Silhouette Reader Service
U.S.: 3010 Walden Ave., P.O. Box 1325, Buffalo, NY 14269
Canadian: P.O. Box 609, Fort Erie, Ont. L2A 5X3

Detective Daddy

JANE TOOMBS

Silhouette

SPECIAL EDITION®

Published by Silhouette Books

America's Publisher of Contemporary Romance

SILHOUETTE BOOKS

ISBN 0-373-24602-1

DETECTIVE DADDY

Books by Jane Toombs

Silhouette Special Edition

Nobody's Baby #1081
Baby of Mine #1182
Accidental Parents #1247
Designated Daddy #1271
Wild Mustang #1326
Her Mysterious Houseguest #1391
The Missing Heir #1432
Trouble in Tourmaline #1464
Detective Daddy #1602

Silhouette Shadows

Return to Bloodstone House #5
Dark Enchantment #12
What Waits Below #16
The Volan Curse #35
The Woman in White #50
The Abandoned Bride #56

Previously published under the pseudonym Diana Stuart

Silhouette Special Edition

Out of a Dream #353
The Moon Pool #671

Silhouette Desire

Prime Specimen #172
Leader of the Pack #238
The Shadow Between #257

JANE TOOMBS

lives most of the year on the shore of Lake Superior in Michigan's Upper Peninsula along with a man from her past and their crazy calico cat, Kinko. In the winter, though, they all defect to Florida for three months. In addition to writing, Jane enjoys knitting and gardening.

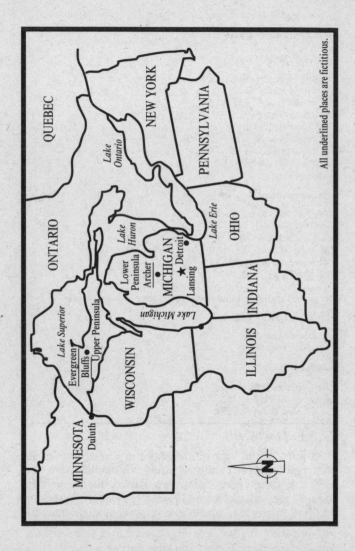

All underlined places are fictitious.

Chapter One

Listening to the howl of the wind outside the hunting lodge in Michigan's Upper Peninsula, Dan Sorenson dropped another log onto the fire and poked it into place. A good night to be indoors, he thought. These storms usually lasted up to three days, switching back and forth from sleet to snow, until they finally petered out. Hell to try to drive in them or to venture out at all. Lucky he'd piled enough wood into the back shed before this particular April storm began.

He glanced around at the comfortable, if shabby, main room of what had been his grandfather's, then his dad's hunting lodge set in acres of wilderness. Its cedar logs had been carefully notched into place long ago by immigrant craftsmen from Finland; the place could stand up to whatever Mother Nature threw at it. Favoring his left leg, he crossed to a side window in a vain effort to peer into the darkness.

He checked the switch to the porch light, left in the up position and shook his head. He'd turned the light on, the same way his mother always had done in a storm.

"You never know who might have need of a light in bad weather," she'd always said.

Certainly no one in this isolated area. But, somehow, he couldn't bring himself to shut it off. He turned away, about to head back to the comfort of the Morris chair drawn up by the fireplace when he was startled by a noise.

Was someone at the door—on this miserable night in the middle of nowhere? Impossible. And yet he was almost sure he'd heard a sort of scrabbling sound, all but drowned by the wailing wind. Better check it out. He turned back toward the door, automatically reaching for his gun. Once a cop, always a cop, but, of course he wasn't wearing his piece, he'd left it up in the loft. Didn't need to keep it on him here in the wilderness, especially during a storm. He reached for the knob and pulled the door toward him.

Dan caught his breath. A woman covered from head to toe with snow stood swaying on the front porch. He reached out and hauled her into the lodge, shoving the door shut against the thrust of the wind.

"C-c-cold," she whispered.

He guided her toward the fire, and took off her soaked coat. My God—the woman was pregnant! She hugged herself, shivering.

"S-so c-cold," she repeated.

Dan convinced her to take off her sweater, but had to help, since her fingers shook so badly. He was concerned to find that the shirt she wore was also damp. So were her pants.

"You need a hot shower right away."

She stared at him so blankly he was afraid she was in beginning hypothermia. "Come with me," he said, taking her chilled hand and leading her into the bathroom.

"I'll start the water," he told her. When he released her hand, she stood where he'd left her, her face expressionless. He was about to tell her he'd get out of the room so she could peel off her wet clothes, but she didn't seem to move.

"Are you able to get undressed without help?" he asked bluntly.

The woman didn't answer.

He pushed out a frustrated breath. "Look," he said, "my name is Dan, and I'm going to have to help you take that shower. Okay?"

He started the water, testing the temperature until it was good and warm, then he pulled her shirt over her head. She didn't react so he turned his attention to the elastic-waist pants that were pulled over the huge bulge in her abdomen. He put down the lid of the toilet, eased her onto it, then removed her shoes, socks and the pants, leaving her in a pair of underpants and a bra that seemed dry.

As he unhooked her bra, he realized just how cold her skin was to his touch. Half-frozen. Where the hell had she come from? He quickly took off her panties, then stood her up and urged her into the shower. Because he worried she might collapse, he stayed in the bathroom watching her as she stood under the running water.

When he judged the water had warmed her, he turned off the faucets, took her hand and led her out of the stall, drying her off with a towel, then wrapping another around her. He led her back into the main room by the fire then he ran up the stairs to his loft bedroom and rummaged through an old cedar chest to find something dry for her to wear. Flannel. Yes, that would do.

He put his grandfather's old flannel pajama top on her, trying not to touch her full breasts as he buttoned it down the front. His grandfather had been a tall and heavy man so the top hung almost to her knees. After he rolled up the sleeves for her, Dan said, "I'll sit you down so we can get on the pajama bottoms."

To his surprise this produced a reaction. She shook her head.

"You'd be warmer with them on."

Pain flickered across her face and she crossed her hands over her swollen abdomen. "It's coming," she said.

"It?"

"The baby."

Dan swallowed. "Are you sure?"

She nodded.

He stared at her, trying to come to terms with the realization that he was the only one she could depend on for help. No, wait, there was his doctor brother in Evergreen Bluff. He couldn't get her there but he could call Bruce and ask him what the hell to do.

Leading her to the old couch that was angled to face the fire, he settled her there, saying, "Take it easy, okay?"

He strode to the wall phone. As he reached for it, the lights went out. He lifted the receiver to his ear and confirmed even more bad news. No dial tone. The phone line was down as well as the electric line and unfortunately, his cell phone didn't work in this remote place.

"Don't worry," he said, as much to himself as to the woman. "I'll light a couple of lanterns."

With the light from the fire guiding him, he soon had two of the kerosene lamps lit. He placed one on the all-purpose table in the main room and set the other on an end table next to the couch. He could see her huddled over, hands clutching her abdomen.

"Hurts," she said.

Damn. He knelt on the floor beside the couch, his mind scrambling to retrieve what he'd learned in the medic classes he'd taken when he first joined the Archer City Police Force. Childbirth had been briefly included.

"As I said before, I'm Dan," he told her. "Dan Sorenson. Can you tell me your name?"

She looked directly at him, seeming to actually see him for the first time. "Fay. Fay Merriweather. Thanks for—" she fluttered her hands in the air "—taking me in and all."

He smiled at her. "Hello, Fay. Now tell me, is this the date when you expected the baby to arrive?"

"No, it's about two weeks early."

Dan took care not to show his relief. At least the baby wouldn't be one of those real tiny, fragile premature babies.

Dan culled his mind for other questions he was supposed to ask. "Fay, have you been under the care of a doctor?"

"Yes." She sighed. "He didn't want me to drive to Duluth. I should have listened."

That made two of them who wished she had. Probably three, if he included her.

"You don't happen to be a doctor, I suppose?" she added.

"Sorry, no. I'm a cop."

"You must have delivered babies before then." She sounded relieved.

He nodded, with no intention of telling her it had been once only, and that the baby had more or less arrived on his own. The ambulance had shown up quickly and swept mother and child off to the hospital, relieving Dan of all responsibility.

Fay moaned. "Here comes another contraction."

"I think you ought to be lying down," he said.

She didn't reply for several moments, then straightened up, took a deep breath and said, "In my prenatal classes, they said to put plastic under you if you find you're going to have an emergency delivery. Plastic and some old towels or something you can throw away after."

He fervently wished it already was after. "And I'll get a blanket while I'm at it."

"An old one," she called after him as he strode toward the storage cabinet in the back shed.

He was grateful she'd warmed up enough to be coherent, because he was going to need all the help he could get. It'd be a hell of a lot easier to psych himself into confronting an armed perp than to face delivering a baby.

Armed with a plastic drop cloth, and a stack of worn-but-clean towels, he went back and prepared the couch the way Fay had told him. He then returned to the loft and brought out an old quilt from the cedar chest. Back in the main room, he found Fay pacing slowly back and forth.

"Ready," he told her. "You can stretch out."

"Thanks. I know I'm supposed to keep active as much as possible as long as I can, but I really feel exhausted." She settled onto the couch, arranging a throw pillow under her head, but leaving the quilt folded on the top of the couch back. Looking up at him, she said. "If I hadn't seen your light…" Her words trailed off and she began to take deep breaths.

"Another contraction?"

She nodded, and he knelt beside her again, this time tentatively resting his hand on her abdomen. Through the cloth of the flannel top, it felt rigid as a board. He checked the second hand of his watch, watching until the rigidity subsided. Before he could remove his hand, something thrust against it, surprising him. Damned if the baby hadn't kicked him. The realization made him smile. Feisty little thing.

Fay smiled faintly in return. "I guess you felt that kick."

"Let me put the quilt over you."

"The fire is keeping me nice and warm." She turned her head to stare into the flames. "I love wood fires."

He decided this might be the time to find a knife and some string, wipe them as clean as possible with alcohol and have them handy when the need arose. By the time he returned he'd made up his mind not to tell her that he'd do his best to make sure she and her baby would be okay.

The most reassuring thing he could do for her was to keep his mouth shut about how inexperienced he really was. The more confidence she felt about his ability, the less frightened she would be. Strange how people assumed cops delivered lots of babies.

"What happened out there? Lose your way in the storm?" he asked.

"When it got really bad, I must have taken a wrong turn."

"That can happen. You're a long way off the route to Duluth."

"Then the car skidded and I hit a tree," she said. "The airbag stunned me for a bit." She crossed her hands over her abdomen. "At least the baby seems to be all right."

"As long as she can kick she must be."

Fay raised an eyebrow. "She?"

He shrugged. "Don't know why I said that."

"Most men would have said he. They all seem to want sons."

Since Dan didn't want a son or a daughter, raising children in today's world being too chancy, he didn't comment.

"Or else they don't want either a boy or a girl." Her words almost made him feel she was reading his mind, but the bitterness threading through them told him she wasn't thinking of him at all.

"Your—" he began, then changed what he'd been about to say. Since a lot of mothers today were single parents, he wouldn't ask about a husband. "The baby's father?"

"Dead."

"I'm sorry." Uncomfortable now, he decided to stop asking personal questions. "We'll need something to put the baby in once she's born."

Fay smiled slightly. "She, again. I bought a baby bed, one of those you strap into a car, but that's where it is—in the wrecked car along with other baby stuff. And mine, too." She glanced at a window and shook her head. "You can't possibly go out into that horrible storm. So we'll need something temporary."

His gaze fastened on the handcrafted wood-box his grandfather had made to hold his logs and kindling. He rose, strode to the fireplace and dumped the contents of the box onto the floor.

"Once I clean this up, we'll have our temporary crib," he said.

"Looks fine to me. Have you thought about diapers?"

Diapers? Naturally not. As far as he knew most babies wore disposable ones these days. Which didn't help in the here and now. "I saw a stack of old flannel sheets in the cedar chest. I can line the wood-box with some, and I could cut up some for diapers and others for baby blankets."

"Good idea."

He handed her his watch so she could time her own contractions, while he went to fetch the sheets.

Coming back, he cleaned the wood-box carefully and lined it with a flannel sheet, using two more folded for a pad at the bottom. While he worked he kept glancing worriedly at Fay. Finished, he settled the padded box near the fireplace for the heat to warm it, trying to imagine a newborn baby nestling inside. He couldn't.

Shaking his head, he brought the flannel sheets he meant to cut up back to where Fay lay on the couch, pulled a chair over and sat next to her. He started to ask her if she was okay, then noticed that, her face tense, she was timing a contraction. Finally she sighed and relaxed.

"How long did that one last?" he asked. When she

told him, he realized the contractions were lasting a little longer each time.

For several minutes she watched him pile the pieces of cloth onto the coffee table he'd pushed aside. "I'm certainly inconveniencing you," she said finally.

"Emergencies are what cops are for." He reinforced his words with a smile. Poor kid, she needed all the reassurance he could dig up.

"I'm so glad—" she paused, wincing. "Another one. Really powerful."

A minute or two later, she said, "Um, Dan?"

"What is it?"

"I didn't have a partner for my birthing classes. If I tell you what to do, would you mind holding my hand and helping me breathe the right way?"

Between contractions, she explained his role. He edged the chair closer, took her hand in his and breathed with her. "You're doing fine, Fay. We'll get through this together."

"Together," she murmured and then moaned, caught up in a contraction he thought would never end.

"Come on, breathe with me," he told her.

Damn. He figured that pretty soon he'd have to do more than put a hand on her abdomen and that scared the hell out of him. The baby's head comes out first, he reminded himself. Normally face down. That's when he was supposed to tell her to push. He thought he remembered the instructor saying to try not to let the baby pop out too fast because it might injure the mother. He gritted his teeth, unsure of how to prevent that. Tell her not to push?

When the contraction ended, he got up, hurried to

the phone and lifted the receiver. Still dead. As it undoubtedly would be until the storm was over. He straightened his shoulders. Okay. It was up to him. He could do this. He'd never failed an assignment yet. He'd never had one this tough, though.

"You're limping," Fay said.

To think she'd noticed with as much strain as she was under. "My leg's almost healed," he said.

Her contractions came closer and closer together. "I think something's leaking out," she said after the last one. She'd already put her knees up, with her feet flat on the couch, legs spread apart.

"I feel like pushing." She gritted the words out.

He didn't want to keep the baby from coming out, but he placed his hand against the opening as she pushed.

Fay's breathing came in gasping grunts now and he took his hand away and saw the baby's head. He then caught the baby as it slid out.

But something wasn't right. She wasn't crying. Was she breathing? The instructor's voice came back to him. "Hold the baby upside down, insert your little finger in its mouth and extract any mucus that might be blocking the baby's airway."

Holding his breath, he followed through. A glob of mucus dribbled from the baby's mouth, she coughed, then emitted a tiny wail. A moment later she was howling full throttle. He expelled his breath in a great sigh of relief.

"She's a girl," he told Fay as he laid the baby on her abdomen.

Fay raised her head to look at her daughter and smiled. "Isn't she beautiful?"

"She sure is," he answered absently, alarmed anew at the amount of blood soaking the towels.

"Is it all over?" Fay asked after a minute or so.

"Not yet."

"In my prenatal class, they said the nurse would massage my abdomen after the baby was born to help expel the afterbirth."

Dan was willing to try anything. He slid the baby higher up on Fay, and as gently as he could, he began to massage Fay's abdomen.

"I think you have to do it harder," she said.

He increased the pressure. The afterbirth came out and the blood flow diminished. But it seemed to him she'd lost quite a bit. A lot more than that woman who he'd helped deliver her fifth child. Too much?

"All over," he told her.

Once he'd tied off the cord and severed it, he wrapped the baby girl in one of the small blankets he'd cut and lifted her cautiously, supporting her along his left arm while holding her there with his right. He eased her into the wood-box and returned to Fay.

"Got to get you cleaned up," he told her. "I'll let the back of the Morris chair down and carry you over there while I fix up the couch. You'll be able to look into the crib from there."

As she watched him, she said, "I don't think I've ever seen a chair like that. It's sort of like a lawn chair but made of wood."

"Really old—my grandfather's."

"Put plastic over it first."

Dan obeyed, then lifted her into his arms, surprised at how light she felt. Once she was settled into the

Morris chair, he disposed of everything that had been on the couch.

"I wish I felt strong enough to clean up my baby," she said when he returned. "I'm pretty well out of commission right now, though."

"Don't worry about it. After what you've been through, you need to rest."

Her gaze met his and, for the first time he noticed that her eyes were hazel, somewhere in between green and brown. Her pallor disturbed him.

"After what *we've* been through," she corrected. "You said we'd do this together and we did."

Her words warmed him as he put new plastic on the couch and covered it with the last of the flannel sheets.

"If you'll get me a basin of water," Fay said, "I'll clean myself up a bit before I go back to the couch." She nodded toward the remainder of the old towels he hadn't used. "If you just put those on the back of the couch so they'll be handy later, when I need them."

Dan busied himself with gently washing the baby while Fay washed herself. When she finished, he carried her back to the couch and she stretched out with a sigh as he covered her with the quilt. He'd no more than turned away, when the baby began crying.

"She may be hungry," Fay said.

Damn. He hadn't even thought of the baby needing nourishment. While there was food enough for him and for Fay, there was nothing for a baby.

"If you'll bring her to me, I'll see if she'll nurse," Fay said.

Stupid of him not to think of that. He was more rattled by all that had happened than he'd thought.

Fay had bared a breast by the time he carried the baby to her and, fascinated, he watched as the tiny girl found the nipple and began to suck. Then, realizing he was staring, he flushed and turned away, muttering, "Sorry."

"I don't mind," Fay said. "Nursing a child is a natural act, after all, just like childbirth."

It was certainly true he found nothing sexual about it. He'd felt privileged to have assisted at a miracle.

Turning back he touched the baby's head lightly with his finger. "She *is* beautiful," he said softly.

As he seated himself in the Morris chair, he realized Fay was also beautiful, something he'd been too distracted to notice until this moment. She was unnaturally pale right now; she wore no makeup, and her dark brown hair hung limply around her face. Still, none of that mattered. Beauty wasn't always a matter of the right clothes, right hairdo or the right makeup.

As for the baby, holding that tiny body had made him understand for the first time his ex-wife's inner need to have a child. There was something about the warmth and helplessness of a baby that triggered something deep within. Yes, even in him, the man who'd vowed never to bring a child of his own into this dangerous and imperfect world.

Chapter Two

Once the drowsy baby finished nursing, Dan carried her back to the improvised crib. When he turned to Fay, he saw her eyes were closed. Good, she needed to sleep. Since neither of them required his help for the moment, he used this chance to duck out to the garage and start the generator. They needed electricity not only for the lights, but for the well pump, so they could have running water. He'd warm the water in the wood kitchen range for bathing the baby and for Fay.

He got into his winter gear, tied a scarf across his face and headed for the back shed. As he opened the shed door, Fay cried out, "Don't leave me!"

He turned and saw her sitting up, staring at him.

"I wouldn't do that." He realized there was more indignation in his tone than reassurance. Didn't she know he'd never desert her?

"You're going out into that storm," she wailed. "What if you can't find your way back?"

"Just to the garage to turn on the generator. We need electricity. The garage is close to the back shed. Believe me, I won't get lost."

Fay watched him step into the shed and close the door, cutting off her view of him. She sank back down onto the couch, clutching her hands over her now deflated abdomen, feeling more tired than she could ever remember. Daniel Sorenson was her lifeline. Hers and the baby's.

She took deep breaths, trying to control what she knew was illogical panic. The emotion was strange to her. Cool, competent Fay Merriweather had always been the one others turned to when things went wrong. She'd never realized giving birth would make her feel so vulnerable. But then she'd never expected to have the baby in a wilderness log cabin during the worst storm she'd ever seen.

In a hospital there were doctors and nurses to take care of everything. Here all she had was Dan. If anything happened to him... She blocked that line of thought.

I have to be strong for my daughter, she told herself firmly. *I* will *be strong.*—which was easier said than done. But Dan would be back, he'd said so. She glanced toward the wood-box that was being used as her baby's bed, and she smiled slightly as she made a decision.

She'd planned on the name Marie if she had a girl, but circumstances had changed her mind. Marie would be her daughter's middle name, not her first. Fay's eyes drooped shut. Half-asleep, she heard Dan reenter the cabin. She sighed and plunged into oblivion.

The sound of a baby's wail roused her. For a moment or two, seeing unfamiliar surroundings, she couldn't place where she was. Whose baby—? Then she heard a man's voice. She turned her head and saw Dan lifting a baby—her baby—into his arms. She could tell it was daylight through the window, but the roar of the wind let her know the storm was still raging.

"You are one wet little peanut," he said in a soft, teasing tone she knew was meant for the baby. "Good thing I got the generator going so I can use the washer, 'cause we definitely have a limited supply of dry diapers. Not to mention baby blankets. And only two safety pins."

She watched as he laid the baby on the table and somewhat awkwardly removed the wet diaper and replaced it with a dry one, then wrapped her in a blanket. He picked her up again and turned toward Fay.

"Good morning," she said.

"In some ways," he agreed. "We're okay, but the storm's still stuck fast in the Upper Peninsula." He crossed to her and handed down the baby who'd begun to cry again. "I think she's saying she's hungry."

"You can call her Marie," Fay told him as she arranged the child at her breast. For a moment, fully occupied with making sure Marie was sucking, then wincing just a little at the cramp nursing brought to her lower abdomen, she wasn't looking at him. When she did, she saw he'd turned so he wasn't facing her.

"Are you all right?" he asked.

Thinking he'd noticed her wince, she said, "Yes. Nursing is supposed to help interior healing."

"That's good."

"You don't have to keep looking away from me while I'm nursing," she told him.

"I know it's a normal process," he said, "but it's new to me."

A tiny giggle escaped her. "New to me, too. It's lucky Marie didn't need to be taught what to do."

He faced her again and nodded. "I—it's sort of a personal thing between mother and child."

Since he was looking at her almost with awe, Fay couldn't help but understand how moved he was by watching her nurse little Marie. She found this incredibly touching.

After the baby finished nursing, Fay felt exhaustion creeping over her again. "Marie needs to be burped," she said. "I don't think I'm quite up to it at the moment. Maybe tomorrow. Could you—?"

Dan blinked. "Burped? How do I do that?"

"You hold her up on your shoulder so any air bubbles in her stomach can rise and come out. Otherwise they might make her stomach hurt."

Fay watched him take the baby from her and position her carefully. It seemed to her each time he held Marie he did so with more confidence. They smiled at each other when they heard a soft but unmistakable burp. As he shifted the baby down to hold her in the crook of his arm, Fay noticed what had accompanied the burp.

"Uh-oh, she spit up a little on your shirt."

"No problem. She couldn't help it." He looked down at Marie, his expression positively doting, which both amused and touched Fay.

As he crossed to lay the baby back in her makeshift bed, Fay threw back the quilt, sat up and plucked one of the old towel pieces from the couch back. She swung her feet to the floor, but when she started to get up, everything whirled alarmingly and she sank back down. Rats. No way could she make it on her own. She was going to need Dan's aid to get to the bathroom and back. As if the poor guy hadn't been already burdened enough.

"Need some help?" he asked, crossing to the couch.

"I'm afraid so. Sorry."

"No need to be. You've been through a lot in the past eight hours."

Once she reached the bathroom, Fay assured him she'd be okay until the trip back. Even if she had to do it by pure willpower alone, she thought. She had a vague memory of him undressing her and putting her in the shower before the baby was born, then dressing her in this way-too-big pajama top. Woozy as she'd been, she distinctly recalled the feel of his warm fingers against her breasts as he'd buttoned the top. The least she could do now was tend to her private needs alone, rather than embarrass them both.

But she was glad of his strength when she leaned against him as he led her back to the couch. He covered her with the quilt and it was all she could do to thank him before she fell into another deep sleep.

By the time Dan gathered up all the wet and soiled flannel sheets and diapers and baby blankets, he had a full load. Thank heaven his dad had installed the small washer with the dryer above it when he'd re-done the bathroom.

If anyone had told me I'd be spending my administrative leave washing baby diapers, he thought, *I'd have asked what he was on.*

He wiped at the wet spot on his shoulder and stared at the few tiny milk curds on his fingers. Fay's breast milk. He took a deep breath. Watching her breast-feed had triggered a strange new emotion, one he'd never felt before. It had nothing to do with lust or sex, but he was damned if he could figure out what it meant. Just like holding the baby and caring for her made him feel as though he'd been awarded some kind of privilege.

Whatever emotion it was unsettled him and he tried to reason it away. So they both needed him. So what. As a cop, plenty of people had needed his skills at one time or another. No reason to get all cranked up about it.

He started the washer, returned to the main room and put another log on the fire. He'd meant to make a meal for Fay, but she was sleeping so soundly he decided to wait. Rest was probably more important than food at the moment anyway. He'd sure hate to go through what she had, especially alone with a stranger in a cabin isolated by a storm.

He thought of his ex-wife and frowned. He couldn't imagine Jean being as brave as Fay under the same circumstances. He stared down at Fay, dark lashes contrasting with too-pale cheeks, her brown hair tangled. Her eyes, he knew, were hazel, a sort of gold-green. She looked so vulnerable asleep, looked as helpless as her baby actually was.

He had no notion of how long it took a woman to recuperate from childbirth. Maybe she'd feel stronger tomorrow, as she'd said.

Little Marie whimpered, and he quickly moved to her side. She wriggled a little, but didn't open her eyes. Blue eyes, he knew. Like his.

Come on, man, he scolded. Probably she had her father's eyes. Besides, hadn't he heard somewhere that babies' eyes changed color when they got a little older?

The fine fuzz on top of her head was blond, also like his. He frowned impatiently. Marie was certainly not his daughter.

That had been one of the reasons he and Jean had gone their separate ways. He didn't want children and she did. Something clutched at his heart as he looked down at the sleeping baby. What a world Marie would face as she grew up, danger lurking around every corner. He wasn't a cop for nothing; he knew what kids had to cope with. None of his would ever have to, that was for sure. But it troubled him to think this little one would.

The next morning, when Fay tried to get up, she found she could make it all the way to the bathroom herself if she held on to furniture or the wall. But she still felt incredibly weak.

"I'll have to ask you to go on taking care of Marie for another day," she told him after she made it back to the couch. "I'm still sort of noodle-kneed."

At his worried look, she added, "But I'm sure it's only temporary." What she meant was she hoped it was only temporary. Still, it had to be, didn't it? "Any sign the storm's letting up?"

He shook his head. "Usually these spring storms are three-dayers. Can last four, but no longer. We're stuck here for a while yet." As he spoke he brought her a tray of food, pulled the coffee table closer to her and set down the tray.

She eyed the toast and eggs with real hunger.

"That gives me at least one more day to recuperate enough to ride into town, then."

"More than one or two. The road's private, so the county plows don't come in here. The plow's still on my truck, though, so I'll get us out to the main road when the time comes. No use starting out from here unless the highway is cleared, and they won't begin 'til the storm's pretty well over. What I can do when the wind dies down is to go look for your car and bring back your stuff. Any idea how far you were from the cabin when you had the crash?"

Fay put down her fork. "I'm not sure. It seemed to take forever to see a light. To get here." Chilled by the realization neither she nor the baby would be alive if she hadn't, she hugged herself.

He reached down and touched her shoulder. "Hey, you made it. Eat up, you need to."

She nodded and picked up the fork, aware he was right. She did need food. Without her breast milk, Marie would have no nourishment. "Thanks. I could use a change of clothes. And I did pack a box of disposable diapers and some baby clothes in the car, too."

She swallowed a forkful of scrambled eggs, then paused. "It just occurred to me to wonder why you left that outside light on in the midst of a storm. Were you expecting someone?"

He shook his head, looking uncomfortable. "A habit left over from childhood, I guess."

"You mean from when your mother left a light on for you?"

"You might say that."

Puzzled, but also curious about his obvious uneasiness, she asked, "Have I said something wrong?"

He released his breath in a sigh before muttering, "At least I had the sense to leave the damn light on."

She'd hit a nerve, though she hadn't a clue why. Somehow she knew, though, it had nothing to do with her.

"Your eggs are getting cold," he told her.

So they were. She picked up her fork again.

Between naps and nursing the baby, the time passed so quickly Fay was surprised to note darkness when she looked at the windows. Dan had run the washer and dryer, so temporarily, at least, Marie had clean diapers and blankets. That evening, after he'd prepared dinner and cleaned the dishes, he pulled a chair up beside the couch where Fay had propped herself up on pillows.

"I'm still curious about how you got here," he said. "Want to talk about it?"

"Just the facts ma'am?" she asked, smiling at him.

"My dad used to watch *Dragnet*," he said. "Police work in those days seemed pretty cut-and-dried."

"My dad watched it, too."

"Was he a cop?"

She shook her head. "He worked as a foreman in an automobile foundry until he retired." When he could have been so much more, she couldn't help thinking. At least she hadn't inherited her dad's lack of ambition. Fay sighed. "I guess you could say my dad is part of the reason I'm here in this cabin. He didn't want me to have the baby."

Dan frowned. "Because your—the baby's father was dead?"

How careful he was not to say husband, Fay told herself, wondering if all cops were so tactful. "You're right in thinking I wasn't married to Marie's father," she said. And that was all she intended to tell him about what had happened there.

"Anyway," she continued, "my mother died five years ago. Since my father and I were at odds, I decided I'd rather have my baby in a more nurturing atmosphere. I still had a couple more weeks to go before my due date, and I made up my mind to drive to Duluth to see my mother's sister and have the baby there. Aunt Marie and I have always been close."

"So she'll be worrying about why you haven't shown up."

Fay shook her head. "Aunt Marie invited me to come stay with her any time I wanted to. She said she wasn't planning on making any trips for a few months and she'd love to have me there. I knew she meant it, which was why I decided to go. I called her to let her know, but when the answering machine started to kick in, I hung up."

"You didn't leave a message?"

"No, I thought I'd call her on the way. You probably think that sounds so impulsive, but that's the way I am."

"You'll get no polite denial from me."

She tamped down her spurt of annoyance. Okay, she had been a tad impulsive. But she'd badly needed someone who cared about her, someone who would welcome the baby. "I did try to call, but my cell phone battery went dead.

"I planned to use a pay phone and I tried that, too, from a gas station near the Straits. But there was only one phone at the place and the guy using it apparently intended to talk forever. The next place I stopped, just before I crossed the Straits, had an out-of-order phone.''

''What you're telling me is your aunt didn't know you were on your way to Duluth.''

She sighed. ''That's one of those Sergeant Friday facts. So Aunt Marie won't be worrying about me.'' Fay eyed him. ''I did plan to call once I crossed the Mighty Mac, but by then it had started to rain and I figured I'd just drive straight through. No need to tell me, I realize it was a bad choice.''

When he raised one eyebrow slightly and seemed about to speak, she tried to change the subject. ''You must have some kind of police rank.''

''Sergeant, just like Friday.''

Though no expert about the police force, she knew sergeants didn't walk beats. ''That makes you a detective?''

He nodded. ''Once over the bridge, the rain got progressively worse, I gather.''

''Yes, but I had no idea it was going to get so bad I got lost.'' She glanced toward the makeshift crib. ''And I certainly had no warning I was going to start labor.''

''The cabin phone's still out,'' he said. ''Can't expect any repairs 'til the storm blows out. And a cell phone won't work in this remote area, so it's just as well your aunt didn't know you were on your way to her. How about your father?''

''I did leave a message on his answering machine saying I was leaving town and didn't know when I'd be back. Not that he cares.''

She fielded Dan's skeptical look and gazed calmly back at him. He had no idea what her father was like. Time to try to turn the tables again. It didn't seem likely he had a wife if he was out here all alone in the wilderness, but he must have relatives. "Isn't there anyone who might be worrying about you?"

"Bruce, Will and Megan, my brothers and my sister, know I can take care of myself. They live in Evergreen Bluff, the closest town to this cabin. We'll be going there as soon as we can get out to the main road. Bruce is a doctor and I'm taking you and Marie to him to be checked out."

"Oh. Well, thanks." She waited a minute, then said, "Do you actually live in this cabin year round?"

"I live downstate, in Archer."

"Archer!" she cried. "So do I. What a coincidence."

As they stared at each other in mutual surprise, she noticed again how bright a blue his eyes were, really an unusual and attractive color. She also saw, for the first time, a thin scar running from his hairline across his left temple. When she realized she was raising her hand as though to touch the scar, she hastily clasped her hands together. What was the matter with her? Had the baby's birth addled her wits?

Marie cried, as if on cue, and Dan hurried to change her and bring her to Fay to nurse.

The next morning, though intermittent snow mixed with rain still sputtered from the clouds, the wind no longer howled around the cabin. After making sure Fay and Marie were all right, Dan set out to try to find the wrecked car. He wished Fay would get some color back in her face. The slow and careful way she walked around the cabin and her frequent naps told him she still wasn't up to par.

He was almost to the creek before he saw the snow-mounded car up against a good-sized pine. He was about to trudge through the snow to it when he noticed the bridge over the creek looked wrong. Wading closer, he let loose with a few choice expletives when he realized what had happened. The no-longer-frozen creek, roiling over its banks with snow melt, had washed out the footings on the far end of the bridge, closest to the main road. Great. Just great. No way to cross the damn thing until it got fixed.

As he slogged his way back to the wreck, he tried to console himself with the fact that at least her car was on this side of the bridge so he had access to supplies for the baby and for Fay. After brushing away some of the snow, it was obvious to him the car would have to be towed when that was possible. It seemed a miracle Fay hadn't been seriously injured.

He wound up making two trips to transport everything he found inside the car to the cabin. On the second trip he thought about Fay wandering lost and half-frozen through the storm. He gritted his teeth, knowing she and the baby might well have died out here, if he hadn't thought of his mother's strange belief about storms and left the porch light on. Though he tried not to think about his mother much, the memory he'd dredged up about the light had saved lives.

But his mother was someone he never talked about, even to his siblings.

"Good thing you brought so much for the baby," he told Fay, once he was inside again. "Looks like we may be stuck here longer than I figured." Then he gave her the bad news about the bridge.

"If it can't be helped, there's nothing we can do," she said, much less upset than he'd thought she would be. "You said there was enough food for us, I have breast milk for Marie, and now we have the stuff from the car. We'll make it all right, the three of us.''

We. The three of us. Her words warmed him even as he tried to push them from his mind. Fay and her baby were his responsibility until he could get the two of them to safety. Still, he was Dan Sorenson, a man who wanted no ties to anyone.

Since Fay was still too weak to trust herself carrying the baby back and forth from the wood-box, Dan continued to fetch Marie for Fay to nurse and, much of the time, to change her diaper as well. He was getting more adept at the latter, especially with the disposable ones. Fay had also included a dozen cloth diapers, which some book she'd read had told her would be welcome in case of an emergency. Dan was sure the author had never figured on this kind of emergency.

He'd thought about and discarded the idea of giving her the only bedroom, in the loft, because he doubted her ability to climb up and down the steep stairs in her condition. Besides, where she was on the couch, near the fireplace, was the warmest spot in the house. Dan had been sleeping in the Morris chair since her arrival since he couldn't take the chance she or the baby would need him in the night and he might not hear from the loft. He'd never felt such a tremendous urge to protect anyone as he did Fay and her baby.

Watching her sleep, he noticed how attractive she looked with her brown hair now softly curling around her face, in the topaz robe that changed her eyes to the same warm shade. He wondered about the baby's father, who'd died, and about Fay's father, who didn't want his own grandchild. He glanced over at the wood-box, where Marie was sleeping. Though he'd recovered the baby bed from the car and set it up, they'd decided together the baby was better off where she was.

"You're frowning." Fay's voice told him she was awake. "Having bad thoughts?"

"Not as bad as some," he told her.

"Yeah, I get those in-between ones. I found the best thing to rid myself of them is to work."

"What kind of work do you do?"

She hitched herself up higher on the couch. "I'm a consultant."

"That covers a lot of ground."

"So do I. After I got my MBA, I worked for a high-powered management company that sent me all over the place doing this and that for different firms. Once I had enough experience, I decided I could do better on my own, so I took the leap and it's worked out great."

"A high-powered consultant."

She smiled and said, "Good description."

"What did Marie's father do?"

"Something similar, only for a firm, not for himself."

"Now *you're* frowning," he told her.

"I like a man to be ambitious. Ken..." Her words trailed off.

"Sorry to pry. A cop gets used to asking questions."

"I don't mind your questions. After what we've been through together we're hardly strangers. It's just that I discovered somewhat late that Ken and I didn't mesh too well. There was no way I could marry him and I told him so."

Dan hid his surprise. "Then he died?"

Fay bit her lip. "I'd already broken off with him by that time. I had no idea then I might be pregnant, but that wouldn't have changed my mind. It was all so sudden, the leukemia he never knew he had and killed him almost overnight." She took a deep breath. "Logically, his death wasn't my fault, but sometimes I feel so guilty." Tears glimmered in her eyes. "Why is it logic has no effect on emotion?"

Dan moved from the chair to sit beside her on the couch and took her hand between both of his. "You can't blame yourself for his disease."

She sighed. "I know. But then, even though I've always used protection, I discovered I was carrying Ken's child and told my father. He insisted I not have this baby. He hated Ken. Dad never reconciled himself to the fact I meant to have my baby." The tears ran down her cheeks.

Dan wrapped his arms around her and held her while she wept, patting her soothingly, trying to ignore how good her softness felt against him.

When her tears eased, she drew away, wiping her eyes with a tissue from the pocket of her robe. "Sorry. It should have been Aunt Marie listening to all this, but I didn't make it that far."

"I don't mind being her substitute," he told Fay. "Not at all."

Only later did it alarm him how much he'd relished being the one who'd offered her comfort in the circle of his arms. It wouldn't do. Not at all. The situation was only temporary. Once they could leave the cabin, she'd go her way and he'd go his. Unencumbered, in his case. Alone.

Chapter Three

By the following day, Fay felt strong enough to pick up little Marie, change her diaper and carry her to the couch to nurse. Every so often, though, she had to ask Dan to carry the baby back to the wood-box, making her wonder if it was normal to have such little exercise fatigue her so.

"The plows should be clearing the highway so repair trucks can get through," he told her in the afternoon. "The problem is I don't know where the electric and phone lines went down so I can't tell how long it'll be before we get them fixed. We're stuck here 'til I can get a call out about the bridge being impassable."

"Now that the storm's over, won't your siblings worry if they don't hear from you?" she asked.

"Bruce might not, and Will's out of town, but Megan's sure to. We tease her that her mission in life is to mother the world. That's why I'm out here. She drove me crazy fussing over me at our old home in town. Seemed to think I needed bedside nursing.''

His words reminded her she'd noticed he favored his left leg when he walked. ''Were you injured?'' she asked.

He shrugged. ''Got shot in the leg. Flesh wound. Pretty well healed now.''

''Is that why you're in the Upper Peninsula instead of on duty in Archer?''

''Some of the reason, anyway.''

Fay was sure the leg wound had been more serious than he let on. She wondered what else was keeping him off duty, but didn't probe. If he wanted to tell her, he would. But he'd made her curious. ''Who shot you?'' she asked.

''The perp. Perpetrator. That's cop talk for the bad guy.''

She opened her mouth to ask what happened to the perp, but decided she was doing exactly what she'd told herself she wouldn't—probing. ''Evidently your job has its exciting moments.''

''Some a lot more exciting than I'd like. Jean—'' He broke off abruptly.

''Jean?'' she echoed.

''My ex.''

''Oh.'' She should have known a guy as attractive as Dan would have been married. At first she hadn't thought of him as anything other than the man who'd saved her life. Who'd taken care of her and Marie. But there was no denying blond, blue-eyed Daniel Sorenson was a hunk to set women's hearts—and other parts—throbbing.

Not that hers were. Physically and emotionally she

was nowhere near ready for either romance or sex. Still, she did have eyes, after all, and she did like to look at him. She also wanted to know more about why Jean was his ex. Well, it wouldn't hurt to ask. "So you're divorced," she said as casually as she could.

His mouth twisted. "Cops' marriages have a tendency to fail."

Fay blinked, having never thought about it before. "Why?"

"We sometimes get killed."

She examined his blunt words. "I admit that's a real problem, but—"

"Cops also work overtime and often can't let a wife know they won't be home on time. The uncertainty of whether their husband might not be coming home because he's dead or lying in a hospital wounded seems to wear on women."

"Okay, but that still doesn't seem to me to—"

"In my case there was also the question of children."

"Question?"

"I don't want any. Won't have any. Not with today's world like it is. Jean wanted kids."

Fay thought of his gentleness with little Marie and felt a pang. She could tell he'd already grown fond of her daughter. Dan would make a wonderful father.

"That's too bad," she said. "Raising a child has always been a risk, though."

"Yet you took it."

She smiled. "I've been a risk-taker for most of my life."

He grinned wryly. "You're not telling me anything I don't know firsthand."

"I guess I deserved that. Going back to your divorce. Do you feel it was your fault? Because I don't. Jean must have known you were a cop when she married you."

"She thought she could convince me to get into something she considered safer. You may have the same trouble understanding what she never could. I like what I do. Once in a great while, I might even make a difference. I don't want to find other work, safer or not. No, I don't blame myself for the divorce, but I do for the marriage. Cops have no business marrying. Especially this cop."

His tone was so bitter she suspected something else was involved at the root of the problem. Deciding not to touch on that, she said, "I think I can understand why you joined the police." Though it was true he'd advanced to detective, he seemed to be saying he liked it just where he was. If he had any ambition, he could eventually become a police commissioner somewhere, become a real power. It reminded her of her father staying a foreman all his life when he could have advanced. He'd liked his job, too.

"We both have reservations about marriage," she added. "How can one ever be sure the other person is the right choice?"

"By steering clear of the whole process in the first place. Like Bruce and Megan."

"Your brother and sister aren't married?"

Dan shook his head. "Bruce claims he knows when he's well off. And Megan says she gets along just fine being single." After a moment he asked, "Ever play double solitaire?"

She realized the question meant the marriage discussion was at an end. "I know what solitaire is," she said, "but I didn't realize two could play it together."

"Not exactly together. More like opponents, since only one can win. I'll teach you later, after your nap."

The word nap made her realize how fast fatigue was once again creeping up on her. She yawned and nodded. Later was fine with her.

Several hours later, Fay had mastered the rules of the game and Dan had beaten her three times out of three.

"Be warned," she advised. "No one wins against me forever."

"You haven't tangled with me before."

"Hey, when I say no one, I mean no one. Just you wait. If you've got a Scrabble board around here someplace I'll take *you* three out of three."

"I'll believe that when I see it."

She smiled. He was in for a big surprise.

Just before Fay fell asleep that night, it occurred to her how fast time was passing. Maybe it was because much of her time was spent either nursing or otherwise caring for her baby and a lot of the rest sleeping, but she was surprised to realize that she wasn't in the least bit bored. Even if the cabin had TV the electricity was out. It was a welcome change not to be reminded of the world's problems.

The batteries in Dan's radio had given up the ghost the day after Marie was born, so the outside world couldn't invade the cabin at all.

They were suspended in a cocoon where time didn't matter. Of course, like all time-outs, it wouldn't last, and, in a way, she was sorry.

* * *

The next morning, Fay woke to the welcome smell of coffee and found sunlight brightening the room. Fire crackled in the fireplace, a sure sign Dan had placed a new log on. She'd never before realized how a wood fire warmed the spirit as well as the body. She said as much to him.

He raised an eyebrow. "Could it be high-powered consultants don't have time to spend contemplating a fire?" She scowled at him and he laughed, adding, "We're out of eggs, out of bread and almost out of peanut butter. The powdered skim milk's still with us, though, so we're having oatmeal for breakfast."

"Is that a tricky way to get me to admit I'm glad I got rescued by a cop who can cook? I'm not such a bad cook myself, as I'll show you one of these days."

After making her way to the bathroom and dressing in a pair of her old maternity jeans, she pulled on a sweatshirt and came over to check on Marie, who was sleeping peacefully. Fay's burst of energy began to fade, but she sat down at the kitchen table rather than retreat to the couch. She simply had to get back to normal.

She dug into the honey-sweetened oatmeal diluted with reconstituted skim milk and ate with relish. "One thing about nursing," she said. "It keeps a gal hungry."

"Good thing the storm's letting up, 'cause that's the last of the honey, too. Tomorrow we're reduced to plain white sugar."

She rolled her eyes. "Horrors."

"The highway must be completely clear by now, so I figure Megan'll be sending someone to check on us today."

"But the bridge is out. Right?" Before he could answer, she said, "Oh, I see what you mean. As soon as whoever it is reaches the far end of the bridge, he'll discover what the problem is—and voilà—we'll be rescued."

"More or less. With luck we'll be out of here by late tomorrow or sometime the following day. Before we're reduced to beans and canned stew."

After Marie's next nursing, Fay napped and roused when she heard what sounded like a truck horn in the distance. Dan was already donning his jacket.

"Going down to greet our rescuer," he told her.

After he left, she got up and peered from a window, but the drive curved among the pines, making it impossible to see what was happening. The rain had melted some of the snow and the sun was trying to finish the job. Here in the woods, though, the trees' shade slowed the melting. She gazed out at what was still a winter scene. In April.

She remembered one of her father's sayings and repeated it aloud. "Spring's like love, it can be delayed, but you can't stop it."

What was he thinking now? Did he worry about where she was and if she was all right? Probably not, he'd be too busy with his new companion, a widow he'd met at Archer's senior center. Fay hadn't met her yet. Hadn't wanted to. Didn't want to.

Restless, she sat at the table and wished she had her laptop computer with her. She hadn't brought it along, figuring she wouldn't be using it at her aunt's. If only she had her computer and a place to plug into a phone line that worked, she would at least know what was going on in the world. Not that it really mattered at the moment. But everything you wanted to know could be found on the Internet.

Well, not exactly everything. Advice might be available on the Net, but advice frequently didn't work when dealing with tricky human relationships. Love, for example. She'd never been quite sure she'd ever actually been in love. Her father's homily said love couldn't be stopped. Okay, but how could you tell when it finally got to you?

The front door opened and Dan stuck his head in. "I've arranged for the bridge to be fixed. Frank's plowed from the highway to the far side of the bridge and he thinks they can shore it up tomorrow morning. I'm going to plow the drive from here to the bridge now so we'll be set to go once the bridge is safe to cross over." Before she could answer, he was gone.

Frank must be the rescuer Megan had sent, Fay told herself. So tomorrow they would be leaving the cabin, all three of them. She sighed, wondering why she didn't feel more elated at the rescue. Probably because she felt so tired. The mere thought of trying to drive home exhausted her. First she would have to arrange for a car, because Dan had said hers was pretty well totaled and would need to be towed. He'd told her he would take care of all that, but she knew the drive would be her responsibility.

Marie began to fuss and, as Fay changed her and settled with her on the couch to nurse, she considered the idea of heading on to Duluth instead. It wasn't any farther from here than going home, and there she'd have her aunt to help her, while in Archer she had no one.

When Marie was satisfied and had been burped, Fay laid her across her lap and studied the baby's tiny features. She envisioned someday telling her daughter the circumstances of her birth. She could end by saying Marie's blue eyes reminded her of the wonderful man who'd saved both their lives.

Nothing about the baby reminded her of poor Ken, but she thought Marie looked a bit like baby pictures she had of her mother, though the blond hair was Dad's and so were the blue eyes.

When she got to Duluth, she'd ask her aunt who she thought the baby resembled. If she made it that far. Fay shook her head. Of course she would. Tired or not, she had to.

Though cheered somewhat by the thought of being with her aunt, it didn't make her feel any stronger. What if Dr. Bruce found something seriously wrong with her when he examined her tomorrow? No! She wouldn't worry about the day that hadn't yet come. After all, this was her first child. For all she knew, her fatigue was normal.

When Dan came in through the back door, he shed his snow gear and found Fay propped up on the couch, the baby asleep in her lap. He eased himself down next to her, saying "We're all set."

He looked at the baby and smiled. "She gets prettier every day."

Fay touched her hair self-consciously, aware she looked far from her best. She knew he'd seen her at what was undoubtedly her worst, but, still, she wished she felt more like fixing herself up. As it was, she'd just run a brush through her hair and hadn't bothered to use any makeup because she hadn't the energy.

Glancing at her, Dan added, "Must take after her mother."

Suddenly Fay realized that he meant the baby's prettiness came from her.

"Nice try at being gallant, Sergeant," she said.

He frowned at her. "I'm not the gallant type. When I say something, I mean it."

He couldn't possibly, not the way she looked at the moment.

"I didn't find a camera in your car," he said.

"I forgot it. I was going to get a disposable one in Duluth."

"My camera's back in Archer. Buying a disposable one's a good idea so you can take some shots of the baby. We can pick it up in town tomorrow."

"What I'd really like is a shot of you holding Marie," she admitted. "One I could show her when she's older, so she'll know who you are." As she spoke, it occurred to her that she wanted the photo for herself, too. So she could look at it and remember. Not that she'd ever forget Dan.

"I've been thinking I'd like to go on to my aunt's in Duluth once I leave here," she added.

He scowled. "You're in no condition to drive anywhere alone yet."

She had to be, there was no choice.

"Why not wait till my brother examines you before making any decisions?"

"Sooner or later, I have to—"

"Later." His tone offered no room for argument. Plucking Marie from her lap, he carried the baby to her bed.

Fay was too tired to bristle. Sighing, she eased herself down and closed her eyes.

As Dan looked over the dwindling food supply, he told himself it was a damn good thing they would be leaving the cabin in the morning. He had enough spaghetti for supper, but nothing to make a tomato-based sauce with. He located some fairly ancient cheese and decided with flour, skim milk and the last dab of butter, maybe he could conjure up an edible white sauce. There would be nothing but beans for a side dish. When he'd stocked up, he hadn't counted on either the storm or the pregnant woman lost in it.

In another way, though, he hated to leave the cabin. In ordinary circumstances he tended to be close-mouthed. The circumstances of Fay's arrival and their enforced intimacy had certainly loosened his tongue. He'd never before explained to anyone why he and Jean had split. Rather than being sorry he'd told her as much as he had, he felt they'd exchanged confidences. He'd shared some of his past with her in the same way she had with him. He was going to miss her. And the little peanut as well. He'd had no conception of how quickly a baby could carve a niche in the hardest heart.

He tried not to worry that Bruce might find something seriously wrong with Fay, but her pallor made him doubt that her lingering fatigue was normal.

Supper, while not an outstanding success, was edible. There was nothing wrong with Fay's appetite anyway. While he cleaned up the kitchen, he glanced now and then at her as she nursed the baby, enjoying the warm feeling it gave him.

After returning Marie to her bed, Fay sat at the table. "Look what I found in one of the cabinets," she said, tapping a finger on what he saw was a Scrabble board. "Prepare for an ignominious defeat."

He laughed. "Only in your dreams, gal."

He hadn't played Scrabble since he'd been a kid, and even then it hadn't been his favorite pastime. But, hell, there wasn't all that much to the game.

When he drew the *X,* worth eight points, right off, he smiled. Since he had an *S* and an *E* he spelled out sex on the board.

His smiled faded as she added a *Y* to the word and spelled yazoo down the other way. "Is that a word?"

"Certainly. It's a person who lives by the Yazoo River in Mississippi."

"Then it'd be capitalized."

"Actually, no, it isn't," she said smugly.

He eyed her assessingly. Was Fay a cheat? Shaking his head, he muttered, "Have to admit I never saw a sexy yazoo. But then I've never been to Mississippi."

The next word he spelt out was breast. As he looked up from the word, his gaze traveled over Fay's T-shirt and, noticing the sensual curve of her breasts underneath, he felt a sudden stir of desire. He wondered why watching her nurse Marie didn't turn him on, yet the sight of her covered breasts had done just that.

You're losing it, Sorenson, he told himself. *Cabin fever.*

In the end, Fay beat him by a narrow margin.

"Close, but no cigar, as my dad used to say," she remarked as she tallied up the game.

"Mine, too," Dan told her. "He said it came from carnivals where you got a cigar if they couldn't guess your weight within a pound either way."

"Do you think we're doomed to become our parents?"

"I sure hope not."

"My mother was okay," she said, "but my dad..." She broke off.

"The other way around in my family." He hadn't known he was going to blurt that out until he heard himself say it. He saw her interest and groaned inwardly. What was there about Fay that made him reveal more of himself than he ever had to anyone else?

"Can I ask, or are you sorry you said anything and don't want to talk about it?" she said.

"Not much to tell," he said gruffly. "She ran off with another man when I was in college and Dad divorced her. He'd never talk about it, but he was devastated."

"Are both your parents still living?"

"Dad is. Bought a place in Florida. Said he had enough of cold winters. I—we don't know where my mother is."

"How sad."

Dan shrugged. His sympathy had always been with his father. He couldn't imagine living all those years with a woman and then, without warning, having her leave him flat for some other guy. Marriage was vastly overrated.

"Is that why Bruce and Megan have never married?" Fay asked.

"Part of it. Will—that's my older brother—had a failed marriage and so did I. That contributed to our belief that Sorensons are better off single."

"I see. But it'd be interesting to talk to your mother."

He stared at her, frowning. Why in hell would she want to talk to his mother?

"There's always more than one side," she informed him. "Didn't you ever search for her?"

"No!" The word burst from him.

"Sorry. I didn't mean to press on a sore point. Or interfere in what's your business and not mine." She rose from her chair.

When he noticed her clutch at the chair back to keep her balance, he jumped to his feet and put an arm around her to help her back to the couch. His anger was no reason to forget how fragile she still was. Wouldn't happen again. Above all, he meant to keep Fay safe.

He just had no intention of marrying her or any other woman. Even if she'd have him. Which he doubted. Fay had made it pretty clear if she ever chose a husband, he'd be the high-powered, ambitious type. Which didn't even remotely describe Dan Sorenson. Not that he cared.

When he'd eased her onto the couch, she looked up at him and said, "When we get the camera, I'll make sure you get a picture of Marie to keep."

He'd forgotten all about the camera. "I'd like that."

"But not necessarily one of me. Really, I usually look a lot better than this."

He figured he'd give her another try at understanding how he saw her. "You look fine. Too pale, but otherwise—"

"You're a sweetheart to say so."

Which he deciphered to mean she didn't believe a word of it, so he decided she wouldn't believe anything else he might have to say about her appearance. If he admitted that he found her beautiful, she would attribute it to kindness on his part. Gallantry, even.

"There's more than one who'd tell you I don't

have a kind bone in my body," he told her. "Or a sweet heart."

He could see his words had confused her.

"You're wrong about what I want," he added. "I'd like a photo of you as well as one of Peanut."

"Peanut? Is that how you think of her?" She smiled. "I guess she is sort of tiny, at that. Maybe your brother or sister will take one of the three of us. A memento of the April storm."

Megan would, he was sure. A memento. But that was what their time together would become, after all.

Dan reached a gentle finger to brush a strand of hair from her cheek, his touch lingering on the smoothness of her skin for a moment. "Yes," he said. "Something to remember."

He already suspected the hard part would be forgetting.

Chapter Four

By noon the next day, the bridge had been shored up enough for Dan's pickup to cross over safely. With the baby in the car bed fastened into the back of the extended cab, he and Fay set off for Evergreen Bluffs.

He'd helped her pack all her belongings and, along with the baby's, they were stored inside the truck's cabin. As he drove toward town, Dan pushed away the thought of having to say goodbye.

"I can't believe I got off on the wrong highway in the storm," Fay said. "And to make it worse, wandered so far off the highway onto a private road."

"Easy to get disoriented when there's a whiteout," he told her.

"Believe me, I'll be more careful from now on."

"I sure hope so."

"I will. Your attitude changes when you have

someone as helpless as Marie depending on you. I can't afford to be as much of a risk-taker.''

"Tell me."

"I know we're going to see Dr. Bruce. Will I be meeting Megan as well?"

"She'd kill me if I didn't bring you over to the house. She's a high school teacher, so she'll be home later in the afternoon."

"You mentioned another brother—Will? Where does he live?"

"In town, but he's in Lansing at the moment at some kind of legal conference."

"Will's a lawyer?"

"Yeah." After that he couldn't find anything more to say. They were nearing town before he asked, "You doing okay?"

"If you mean am I going to collapse when I get out of the truck, no. But I may have to lean on you, as usual."

"Be my guest."

She glanced at him. "I've already been your guest for the better part of a week. I imagine you'll breathe a long sigh of relief when we're gone."

The words were there, waiting to be said. *I'll miss you.* He held them back. Not because they weren't true, but because he didn't want to admit it. To her. Or to himself.

He had to say something. "You've been good company." Also true.

"But certainly troublesome company."

What was he supposed to say to that? Her arrival sure as hell had been a far-from-welcome complication in his life, but he didn't regret anything that had happened once he'd rescued her. And he certainly didn't regret the rescue. He couldn't bear the thought that Fay and her still unborn baby might have frozen to death in the storm.

When they reached his brother's home/office, Dan retrieved Marie from the back seat, cradling her against him as he helped Fay down from the truck's high seat. She held his arm as they made their way into the building.

Bruce's receptionist, red-haired Wendy, made a big fuss over the baby. "What a little darling," she cooed. Giving Dan a sideways look, she added, "Never thought I'd see the day you'd be carrying a little one around." Shifting her attention to Fay, she said, "Come right in through that door. Doctor's with a patient, but we'll get you nice and comfortable in an examining room while you wait."

Dan followed Fay to the room Wendy indicated. "Want me to stay with you 'til Bruce comes in?" he asked.

She shook her head.

"You can bring the baby into the back office," Wendy told Dan. "Doctor'll want to examine Ms. Merriweather before he looks at her daughter." Turning again to Fay, she said, "I'm going to bring you some forms to fill out while you wait." Shooing Dan ahead of her, Wendy bustled out.

One of the forms, Fay discovered after Wendy returned with them, was the information needed for the baby's birth certificate. She smiled as she wrote down the name she'd chosen: Danielle Marie Merriweather. Perhaps Dan wouldn't mind that she'd named her daughter after him, but she'd decided not to take the chance, so hadn't told him. And wouldn't.

By the time all the forms were filled in, a fortyish

woman entered and set a small tray down on the top of a cabinet. "I'm Ellen, the office nurse," she said. "I'm here to weigh you and take your blood pressure." When she finished, she added, "Doctor Sorenson wants me to get a blood sample, too."

With practiced efficiency, she drew the blood. Eyeing Fay assessingly, she said, "Are you okay? You look kind of pale."

"Just tired," Fay said.

"You'll have to do it sooner or later anyway, so why don't you undress, slip into a gown and get up on the table where you can stretch out?" Ellen indicated a corner with a curtain pull. "The gowns and a sheet to cover yourself are in there." She gathered up the tray and the filled-out papers before leaving the room.

Fay did as the nurse suggested, breathing a sigh of relief when she was flat on the table. Damn this lethargy. She fought to stay awake, but her eyelids were drooping shut when she heard the knock at the door before it opened. The doctor. He looked enough like Dan so she thought she could have picked him in a crowd as Dan's brother, even though he had a slimmer build and his eyes were a lighter shade of blue.

"Hello, Fay," he said. "I'm Bruce Sorenson, Dan's brother." He held out a hand to her and she shook it.

"Thanks for seeing me on such short notice," she said.

He didn't release her hand, but turned it over, peering down at her fingers as he said, "No problem. Dan filled me in a little about what happened after you got lost in that storm and found your way to the lodge.

I'll examine your daughter later. First we'll see about you.''

Letting go of her hand, he leaned toward her, saying, ''I'm just going to pull your lower lid down for a moment.'' He checked one eye, then the other.

''Dan mentioned that you bled quite a bit before delivering the placenta. Any marked bleeding since then?''

''No, not really.''

''From the looks of things, you may have anemia. I can't tell for sure until I take a look at your blood under the microscope, but I strongly suspect that's the reason for the persistent fatigue Dan mentioned to me.''

Fay swallowed. ''You did say anemia, not leukemia?''

''I did. It's not uncommon and is easily treated with medication and diet. Anemia is an entirely different condition than leukemia. There's no connection. You should be feeling your old self in a few weeks, give or take a day here and there.''

''That long?''

''Don't look so alarmed. You need rest, a good diet and medication to bring your count back up and that takes time. I strongly suggest you stay at a place where someone can help you with the baby.''

''My aunt lives in Duluth. I can call her.'' But how was she going to get there alone? Just being a passenger on the short drive here had worn her out.

Someone tapped on the door and Ellen stuck her head in.

''I'm ready to do the exam,'' Bruce said to the nurse, who then entered the room.

Fay prepared herself for the poking and prodding

she knew would come, her attention fixed on the problem of getting to Duluth rather than the exam.

"Everything looks good," Dr. Bruce told her when he finished. "There's no sign of infection, your uterus feels normal and so does everything else. Once we get you over what I suspect is anemia, you'll be fine. When you get home, though, be sure to have your doctor examine you. I would suggest you refrain from sexual intercourse for at least a month. Your own doctor will tell you when you can resume."

Fay felt her face flush with embarrassment. Didn't he realize sex was the last thing on her mind? "I wasn't planning to do anything like that." She could hear the indignation in her voice.

"Good." He smiled at her, then turned and left.

Ellen helped Fay down off the table. "Once you're dressed I'll take you to the back office. Doctor'll want to talk to you after he examines the baby."

Fay found Dan there. "Bruce is taking a look at Marie," he said. "Everything okay with you?"

"He thinks I have anemia," she confessed. "That's why I'm so tired all the time. Otherwise I'm fine. Once he's confirmed the diagnosis, he's going to give me some medication and wants me to eat well and take it easy for a month. As long as I can get to my aunt in Duluth, that'll be no problem."

Dan gestured toward the phone on the doctor's desk. "Call her."

Fay hesitated. "Do you think your brother will mind? I do have a phone card."

"He won't care. Go ahead."

When she reached her aunt's number, Fay heard the answering machine kick in after four rings. Instead of the familiar message about not being able to come to the phone, she heard a different one.

"Please call me at 619—"

Fay forgot the rest of the numbers as she grabbed a pen from the desk and looked for something to write on. Fortunately, her aunt's message repeated the numbers and she scribbled them down.

She hung up and glanced at Dan. "That's a San Diego area code," she told him. "My aunt must be visiting her daughter. Strange, she had no plans to go there." Fay used her phone card to dial the California number.

Aunt Marie herself answered. "Oh, my dear, Fay," she said. "I was hoping you'd call. Gwen was in a frightful car accident and we almost lost her. I flew out immediately when I heard and I'm taking care of the boys and, of course, Roger. Poor man, he's beside himself with worry. Thank the Lord she's improving and they think she'll recover completely in time. I'll be staying right here until she's back on her feet again. How are you doing?"

Realizing she couldn't burden her aunt with any more of a problem than she already had, Fay said, "I'm so sorry to hear about Gwen's accident. I just called to tell you that you have a new niece. Both of us are fine."

"A baby girl! Isn't that wonderful? I'm so happy for you." Aunt Marie went on for a bit, then said goodbye, saying she was heading to the hospital to visit her daughter.

"Give Gwen my love," Fay said and put down the phone.

"So going to Duluth is out of the picture for you," Dan said.

She nodded, wondering what she was going to do.

"You obviously aren't strong enough to drive home yet," he told her. "I'm still on leave for the month of May, so the best solution would be for us to return to the cabin where you can rest and recuperate until your blood count's back to normal, and I can help you take care of the baby."

"You what?" Dr. Bruce asked from the open doorway, his eyebrows raised.

Fay hadn't heard him approach and, obviously, neither had Dan.

"Am I hearing right?" Bruce continued, staring at Dan. "You're actually offering to care for an infant for a month?"

"I delivered her, didn't I?" Dan's tone was gruff.

"You didn't have much choice. Though I have to admit you did okay." He smiled at Fay.

"Ellen will bring your baby to you shortly. She weighs seven pounds, ten ounces and is 20 inches long. All indications are that she's a healthy, normal little girl."

At his last few words, Fay realized she'd been holding her breath, waiting to hear more bad news. She sighed in relief.

"The baby's blood count is normal," Bruce added, "but yours indicates a definite anemia. I'm going to give you an injection right now and then a prescription that you should fill before going back to the cabin, if that's what you decide to do. I want you to call me if you have any new symptoms and come in for another blood count before returning home."

"Thank you," she said.

"I reported the phone and electric lines being

down," Dan answered, "so they'll be getting to them as soon as possible."

Bruce gave Dan a measuring look as he drew liquid from a small vial with a needle and syringe. "Dan, if you want to take on this responsibility, who am I to argue? You seem to have done a fairly decent job of baby care so far and Fay does need to have someone to help her. I do agree it's best if she doesn't undertake a long, tiring trip right now."

"But I don't want to impose—" Fay began.

"It's no imposition," Dan told her. "Think about it. You said yourself there's no one back in Archer to help out. Your aunt is in California, not Duluth, but here I am. Me and the cabin."

She bared her upper arm for the shot, thinking she couldn't argue with what Dan had said. It did seem to her, though, that Dr. Bruce wasn't too keen on his brother taking her back to the cabin. Was there some reason he didn't approve of her? He surely couldn't think she was out to trap Dan into marriage. Ridiculous. Especially in her condition.

The needle pricked through her skin, the injection stinging for a brief moment, but she hardly noticed. Her attention was fixed on why Dan had offered to take care of her and Marie. She'd have thought he'd be eager to see the last of the trouble she and her daughter had caused him. At the same time, she was glad he had offered, even if he'd done it out of a misplaced sense of obligation. She was the one obligated, not him.

It wasn't only that he'd solved her problem. If she were honest, she'd have to admit, she'd rather be with him than to entrust her baby to someone she wasn't sure she could count on.

"That should do the trick," Dr. Bruce said. "Unless something unusual and unexpected occurs, you should notice the difference in about a week. But take the pills, too."

She thanked him again. As they were leaving the room, she saw him exchange a significant glance with Dan.

Sure enough, once Dan had settled Fay and the baby into the truck, he said, "Be back in a minute," and returned to the office.

Brother Bruce warning him about her? But why?

After Dan returned, he drove Fay to his childhood home, a two-story frame house, painted white, with a long front porch shaded by several huge maples that were beginning to leaf in.

Megan opened the front door before they reached it. She hugged Fay, guided her in and insisted she relax on the couch, saying, "You look so pale, you must be exhausted." Once Fay was arranged to her satisfaction, she turned her attention to Dan.

"You carrying a baby," she said. "I never thought I'd see the day."

"Wendy already said that." Dan sounded grouchy.

Megan grinned at him, then asked Fay, "May I hold her?"

Fay nodded, fatigue catching up to her.

Seating herself on the couch next to Fay, Megan cuddled Marie, who screwed up her face and began to wail.

"Peanut must be hungry," Dan said.

Megan made a face at him. "Peanut?" She glanced at Fay. "Do you want me to warm a bottle?"

"No thanks, I'm nursing."

"Would you like to go in a bedroom?"

Fay hesitated, but then shook her head. She didn't hide when she nursed Marie in front of Dan, so why would she hide from his sister? "Right here is fine, if you don't mind," Fay said, undoing her shirt.

"Not at all, but—" Megan broke off and glanced at Dan.

"I take it you think I'm the one who ought to go into a bedroom," he said to Megan. "Come on, Sis, nursing is a normal activity. Marie doesn't mind a bit if I'm present."

"It isn't the baby I—" Megan broke off and frowned at him. "You're teasing me."

"Yes, he is and shame on him," Fay put in. "Seriously, Megan, I'm not bothered by Dan being in the same room. After all, he helped me deliver the baby and has been taking care of her ever since. We're not exactly strangers."

"I'll bring the old cradle downstairs for the baby," Dan told his sister. "Is it still in the attic?"

"No, it's in the back bedroom. I polished it up, had a new mattress made and put my old dolls in it. I figured if none of you three dolts were ever going to get married or stay married long enough to produce an heir, the dolls might as well enjoy the cradle."

Without replying, Dan left the room.

"I shouldn't have said all that," Megan said. "Least of all to Dan. In fact, not at all. Especially since I have no plans to marry either."

"Join the crowd," Fay told her. "I feel the same way."

"But you did produce the heir." Megan's tone was wistful.

"Marie wasn't planned." Fay smiled down at her daughter. "Not that she isn't welcome."

Megan sighed. "She's a beautiful child. I wish you all the luck in the world raising her."

"I'm beginning to realize I'll need all the luck I can get."

"What do you think of Dan?"

"Why, I'm very grateful to him. If he hadn't been there to rescue me..." Her words trailed away as usual when she had to face what could have happened. "I know I took an awful risk, but it didn't seem that way at the time. I think I might have made it all the way to my aunt's if it hadn't been for the storm. The problem with that is she probably was getting the call for help while I was on my way and so would've been on a plane to California."

Seeing Megan's confusion, Fay explained what she'd planned to do and why her aunt had left Duluth so suddenly. "Luckily Dan's a cop and knows how to handle emergencies," she added.

"He's really a great guy," Megan agreed. "All my brothers are, even Bruce who was the youngest of the three and so the closest in age to me.

"I sometimes think that if mother—that is, if things had been different, Bruce wouldn't've had that problem in high school."

"Dan mentioned your mother had left when he was in college."

Megan stared at her, obviously taken aback. "He told you that? Dan, the original zipped lip?"

Fay, uncomfortable under her scrutiny, turned her attention to her daughter, shifting her up onto her shoulder to burp her. Before she managed to think of what to say, Dan came back into the room, carrying the cradle.

"What do you think of it?" he asked, setting the cradle down alongside the couch.

"What marvelous workmanship," Fay said. "Just look at that beautiful wood. You can tell an expert craftsman built it."

"Our grandfather," Megan told her. "Dad could do plain carpentry, but Will's the only one of us who inherited Grandpa's talent—a lot of use that is to him as a lawyer. Grandpa did teach me to whittle, though."

"You still do that?" Dan asked.

She nodded, looking a bit defensive, Fay thought.

"I'll be taking the cradle back to the cabin, if it's okay with you," Dan said. "For the baby. Fay's going to be staying with me out there for a few weeks more—doctor's orders. She needs to rest and have someone help with Marie's care."

"At the cabin?" Megan cried. "Good heavens, she'd be far more comfortable right here. We've got plenty of room and—"

"With you off teaching five days a week?" he pointed out. "I'm the guy with free time here, not you." Despite his reasonable words, Dan's tone held a hint of steel.

Marie gave a distinct burp, diverting his attention to her. He lifted her from Fay's arms. "Wet again, I see," he said to the baby. "Old Dan'll fix that."

"Old Dan will do what?" Megan's words were tinged with incredulity.

"I'm anemic," Fay told her. "It's made me pretty lethargic, so Dan's had to handle most of the baby's care."

Megan shook her head as she watched him change

the baby with practiced deftness before laying her gently in the cradle. "Remarkable."

"She is, isn't she?" Dan said, smiling down at Marie.

Megan glanced at Fay, who shrugged.

Turning to look at Fay, Dan said, "I'm going to pick up that list of supplies we wrote down before leaving the cabin. Why don't you catch a nap while I'm gone?"

After he left, Megan said, "I still think you should stay here. Don't you find the cabin pretty rustic?"

"It's been fine," Fay said vaguely, trying unsuccessfully to suppress a yawn.

"Sorry. I don't mean to argue with you when I can see you need to rest. I think you've been good for Dan. You know he was the middle boy."

"Middle boy?" Fay echoed, not understanding her meaning.

"You know, Will was the oldest, Bruce the youngest, so each got some special attention that the middle child misses. Will was Dad's favorite 'til I came along and Bruce was our mother's. I guess you could say Dan was never anyone's favorite. Am I making sense? All my brothers tell me I talk too much and they may be right."

Fay smiled at her. "I'm not your brothers."

"Well, what I meant was that Dan got to do something really special when he delivered your baby."

"As a policeman, he's done that before."

"Not under the same circumstances. And he certainly never had to take care of a baby before. I can't believe how good he is with little Marie. I'm seeing a whole new side of him. One I like."

In Fay's book, winding up on Dan's doorstep in a

snowstorm to disrupt his life as completely as she had could hardly be classified as being good for him. "He's been very patient," she said. "Patient and kind."

"The brother I know didn't have a patient bone in his body," Megan countered. "As for kind, the less said the better. What I am saying is that what happened changed him. For the better, as far as I'm concerned." She shook her head. "All this talk isn't letting you get any rest. If you need anything, just call. I'll be in the kitchen."

Left alone with the sleeping baby, Fay tried, not too successfully, to fit Megan's words into her own picture of Dan. He'd been more than patient with her and the baby, so it was hard to imagine him any other way. At least Megan seemed to like her and even approve of her. Unlike Doctor Bruce, Megan hadn't acted upset that Dan had offered to help with the baby while Fay recuperated for a few more weeks at the cabin. All Megan had objected to was the cabin itself, offering the house as a more appropriate place.

Fay thought drowsily that, comfortable as it was, she didn't want to be in this house for a month; she wanted to be back in the cabin. Somehow, it felt like home. And, besides, as Dan had pointed out, she'd be alone a lot of time here, while Dan would be right with her at the cabin, ready to help.

Or was it that she'd come to depend on him? The thought made her blink. Too much? She hoped not. She could already see that if she were to stay in this house, the times when Megan wasn't working, she'd be, as Dan had put it, "mothering" her. Fay liked Megan, but she didn't want to be mothered.

Dan seemed to sense when she needed to talk and

when she didn't. They were used to each other. And the baby, too, was accustomed to the way he handled her. She might not take to Megan right away. Marie had already cried when Megan held her.

Fay sighed. Why was she bothering to conjure up so many reasons for not staying in town with Megan? What she wanted to do was go with Dan to the cabin—reasons be damned—and that's what she meant to do. Their time together was short enough as it was.

That last thought troubled her, but she was too sleepy at the moment to examine it and find out why.

Chapter Five

The next morning, when she woke, Fay sat up and looked around the cabin with new interest. Discovering she had a specific reason for her abnormal tiredness, a reason that would soon clear up, had eased her mind.

Next to the couch, Danny Marie was sleeping peacefully in the cradle Dan's grandfather had made. Flames flickered yellow and blue nearby in the fireplace and the sun streaming in the windows suggested that soon there would be no need to keep the fire lit for long.

She glanced up at the loft, where she knew the cabin's only bedroom was, but the blanket folded neatly over the arm of the Morris chair told her Dan was still sleeping there nights rather than in his bed in the loft. Maybe now, with the cradle so close to where she slept on the couch, she could manage to nurse and change the baby when she cried during the night, and Dan could sleep in his bed once again.

Where was he now, she wondered. She padded to a window and looked out, the sunlight warm and welcome on her head and shoulders. She saw him crouched near a tree, apparently removing something attached to it. He wore no jacket, his red sweatshirt a brilliant spot of color in the predominately evergreen landscape. She realized as she stood there watching, how much she enjoyed looking at him. Working. Sitting. Holding Danny Marie.

Granted, there was more to a man than broad shoulders, great buns and Viking good looks, but all that was an attractive plus. She wondered how it would feel to have those hands gently touching her. Not in the same way he held the baby, of course, but in a more urgent, adult wanting...

As if sensing her gaze, he looked up and saw her in the window. She flushed, as if he could see what she'd been thinking. Then she waved; he waved back and jogged toward the cabin.

In a long, old-fashioned, flowered flannel nightgown that Megan had given her, Fay decided she was more than decently covered and so she waited for him to come inside.

"New wardrobe," he commented.

"Not exactly. Megan said it came out of your grandmother's cedar chest in the attic."

"Looks warm, but I don't think it's really you." He grinned at her. "I sort of liked you in my grandpa's old pajama shirt."

"The Sorensons have certainly clothed, fed and waited on me. I owe you all big time."

"You'd have done the same for any of us had we needed help."

Would she have? Fay thought of her all-too-busy schedule before the baby was born and wondered if she'd have been able to interrupt it long enough to try to take care of anyone. When you were aiming for the top, there was seldom if ever any time to spare.

"I'll have breakfast on the table by the time you're dressed," he told her.

"I could help."

He shook his head. "Wait 'til you get some pink back in your cheeks."

As she toweled herself off in the bathroom after her shower, Fay checked her mirror image and sighed. Her face still looked pale and drawn.

She suddenly remembered Bruce's measuring look when he realized Dan intended to bring her back to the cabin. Had Bruce warned him that she might be out to trap a husband? Surely Dan wouldn't take his brother seriously. Hadn't she told him she had no intention of getting married? Whatever he thought, best not to put on much makeup at the moment. Still, she found herself taking extra pains with her hair.

At breakfast she asked him, "What were you doing out there?"

"Removing my target so I can set it up farther away from the house when I practice shooting. Can't afford to get rusty just 'cause I'm on leave, but I didn't want the noise to disturb you or the baby."

"You have your gun here at the cabin?"

He nodded toward the loft. "It's always with me."

No doubt a cop thing. She could hardly blame them since their lives might well depend on their gun. And how well they could shoot it.

"During the storm it didn't occur to me there had to be wildlife in these woods. Anything dangerous?" she asked.

"Not really. Maybe a mother bear if you get between her and her cubs."

Fay glanced toward a window. "You've got bears out here? And I've heard the U.P. has wolves. Is that true?"

"Quite a few packs now. Also coyotes, moose, deer, fox, bobcats, fisher and porcupine. None of them bother humans, usually. Though if you come upon a porcupine, better detour around him 'cause he has no intention of getting out of your way."

"Any chance of running into a mother bear with cubs when I feel strong enough to take a walk in the woods?"

"Pretty remote. Black bears are not very aggressive unless cornered. She'd hear us or smell us a long time before we saw her and she'd herd the kids away from possible danger. The most we'd probably run across is a chipmunk or two and a few chickadees. I tried on that pouch thing you brought along and it fits me, so I can carry Peanut in it instead of you taking on the extra strain."

"Sounds good to me."

That night, with the baby peacefully asleep in the cradle, Fay had said good-night to Dan and had curled up on the couch when, from outside, she heard something. What was it? The sound rose and fell, eerie, compelling.

"What's that?" she asked in a half whisper, even though, somehow, she knew.

"Wolves." Dan answered from the foot of the

stairs, then crossed to the windows. "They sound close. Come look, we may see them."

By the time Fay joined him at the front windows, the wolf chorus had died. The moon was up, waxing toward full, its silver light outlining the darkness of the pines. So swiftly she could hardly trust her eyes, an animal slipped into the moonlight, then another and another until there were five in all. They loped across the front of the house only to disappear again into the trees.

"Wolves," she whispered. "Those were real wolves."

Dan placed his arm over her shoulders. "A wolf pack," he agreed, awe in his voice. "I've heard them before, but this is my first sighting."

Fay, feeling they'd shared something magical, sighed as she stared into the moonlit night. "I'll never forget it."

She looked up at him and saw, in the dim glow of the fire, his gaze fixed on her instead of focused on what was outside.

"Unforgettable," he agreed.

For a faint instant, she held her breath, thinking he might kiss her. Before she could decide whether she wanted him to or not, he dropped his arm from her shoulders and turned away, saying, "Good night again."

She watched him head for the stairs, wondering what she'd have felt if he *had* kissed her.

By the following week, the beautiful weather still holding, Fay decided she was ready for a short walk outside. With Danny Marie bundled into a blanket in the baby pouch Dan wore, they set off. Though the breeze was cool, the warmth of the sun countered it until they came under the canopy of the tall white pines. In the shade, Fay was glad of her jacket. No snow remained near the cabin, but patches shone white here and there among the trees.

"It's May," she said. "Down in Archer, there'll be new spring leaves on the trees and the lilacs will be coming into bloom. I noticed when we were in town that the trees barely have any leaves."

"Spring in the Upper Peninsula is always a month behind." He took a deep breath. "What we've got lots of is fresh air."

A chipmunk raced across in front of them. Fay tested the air, realizing it smelled faintly, but pleasantly of pine and forest duff. How long had it been since she'd taken a walk in the woods? Any woods? She really couldn't count those hurried weekend ski trips to one resort or another.

How quiet it was, the only sounds the crunch of their feet on the brown pine needles, the soughing of the wind in the branches high above and the occasional call of a chickadee. It seemed that she and Dan and the baby were the only ones on the planet.

She wondered where the wolves had gone. Dan had assured her the pack offered no danger to them and that the wolves took care to avoid humans. Seeing them that night had been a wonderful fluke.

She hadn't noticed that they circled back until she heard the sound of an engine and caught a glimpse of the cabin through the trees.

"Megan's car." He sounded resigned. "I knew she'd be out here sooner or later."

"I like your sister," she said.

"So do I, but she—" He paused as though searching for the right words. "She always seems to complicate things."

"It'll be a nice change to have company."

He glanced sharply, saw her smiling at him, and gave her a reluctant grin. "Wouldn't want you getting cabin fever."

"That won't happen until my cheeks are as pink as wild roses. Then look out. At my best I have more energy than you can imagine."

"I can't wait."

What did that look in his eyes mean? Surely not lust. Her appearance right now wasn't likely to inspire that. Besides, Dan had never given the slightest indication he was interested in her in that way. If she didn't count the night they'd seen the wolves...

As they emerged from the trees, Megan spotted them and called out a greeting.

Before they entered the cabin, Megan said, "I saw the phone company truck parked on the highway near your driveway."

"About time," Dan muttered. "I'll head down and see what's going on."

He lifted the baby out of the pouch and handed her to Fay.

Inside, Danny Marie began to fuss when Fay settled her in the cradle.

"Go ahead, take off your jacket," Megan said. "I'll rock the cradle."

By the time Fay was ready to sit on the couch, the baby had quieted. "Would you like a cup of tea? Coffee?"

"Nothing, thanks. I just dropped by to see how you were doing. I'll be glad when the cabin phone is fixed so I can call to see if you need anything."

She gestured toward the picnic basket she'd brought. "I made a casserole and some brownies for you and Dan."

"Thanks, that's great. I'm doing better, but Dan won't let me cook yet. He's a pretty good one, but his dishes are limited."

"He's a stubborn Sorenson, like all the males in the family. There I was rattling around in that big house in town, perfectly willing to help him recover, but he insisted he'd do better on his own and came out here to the cabin. He's still limping, isn't he?"

"A little, though it doesn't seem to bother him much. In fact, I'd think they'd want him to return to duty soon."

"He's on administrative leave. They won't call him back until the investigative committee decides it was okay for Dan to have killed the drug lord who shot him in the leg first." Her tone was scornful. "I mean, you're a cop, someone shoots you, you shoot back. Makes sense to me."

"Me, too, but I suppose it's a regulation to investigate all shootings."

"That's what Dan said. The Archer paper wrote him up as a hero, which he really was. They'd been trying to nail that scumbag for over a year."

Fay wondered how she'd missed all that. Not that she read the local paper regularly. "I guess you could say Dan's my hero, too. Mine and the baby's. We owe our lives to him."

Megan nodded. "So I should quit complaining. It really was a good thing he did insist on staying out here. I've been hoping he'd find someone who wasn't like Jean, someone who—"

Fay held up her hand. "That's not me. Dan tells

me he'll never marry again and I believe him. In any case, I'm not interested in getting married, either. Or, at the moment, in anything except friendship with any man.''

"It's just that Dan acts besotted with your baby."

Fay laughed. "I think so, too. But, believe me, it doesn't follow that he feels that way about the mother. And, as I said, I'm grateful, but that doesn't translate into anything like, well, love, or any type of commitment.''

"I didn't mean to be offensive," Megan said, then sighed. "I guess I'm just a hopeless romantic, like my brother Bruce is always telling me when I turn some guy down who wants to marry me."

"There's nothing wrong with waiting for a man you can love."

"Is that what you're doing?''

"I'm not sure I'll ever find a man I want to marry." Engrossed in the conversation, Fay hadn't heard the shed door open. Apparently Megan hadn't either, because she looked as startled as Fay felt when Dan said, "Now that's what I call a smart woman." He grinned at them as he hung his jacket on a peg.

"I have to be running along," Megan said, rising. "I promised to help with the museum's bake sale. You're in luck, big brother, I brought supper so you don't have to cook tonight."

Dan gave his sister a quick hug. "I knew there had to be some reason you were born," he told her. "Thanks."

As she watched Megan leave, Fay felt a familiar pang, one she'd experienced before when siblings showed their affection for one another. Being an only child might have certain benefits, but it could also be lonely.

"They told me the phone'll be working before dark," Dan said, taking a look inside the basket. "Mmm, brownies. Want one?" He offered her the pan.

Megan had already cut them into squares and the chocolate aroma was too tempting to resist. Fay took one.

So did Dan. He put the pan back and eased down on the couch next to her. "Megan's a good cook," he said after the first mouthful. "Guys are always asking her to marry them."

"But she never does because she hasn't yet fallen in love. Anyway, who wants to marry a man who loves your cooking more than you?" She bit into the brownie and rolled her eyes in appreciation.

"Didn't I just hear you say you may never find a man who suits you?"

"Something of the sort, but you already knew that."

"You've got the baby now."

"So?"

"She'll need a father."

Fay stared at him. "You certainly can't be saying you expect me to marry some guy so she can have a father figure in her life."

"Not exactly, but—"

"Come off it, Sergeant. That may not be the worst excuse for getting married that I ever heard, but it ranks pretty close to 'He needs me.' A friend of mine married a guy she decided really needed her and then found out what he'd actually been looking for was a replacement for good old mom, who'd always done everything for him. Needless to say—splitsville.''

"You must be getting better,'' he said. "We're having our first argument.''

"I am better. Stronger. You must have noticed I don't sleep all the time now.'' As he started to speak, she put up a hand. "And don't start in on how I should rate the only bed in the house. We've already agreed that it's better for me to stay on the couch and you to sleep in the loft.''

"What I was going to say has nothing to do with the bed in the loft.'' Dan said. Which was the truth. When they'd first discussed the matter, he'd refrained from pointing out it was a double bed, big enough for two, but that didn't mean he hadn't thought about Fay sharing his bed with him. Which, of course, was an impossibility. "I was going to ask you if you felt up to going out to dinner on Friday. That's when the Black Bear Lodge serves a mean fish-fry, and it has the best view from its picture window. It's not far from town, so we could leave the baby with Megan for an hour or two.''

She blinked at him. "I, um, don't know. We've never left Da—Marie with anyone before.''

"You told me you were thinking about going back to work part-time once you got home. You'll have to find someone to look after her then.''

"I know, but I hadn't yet gotten around to totting up the logistics of going back to work. It's not that I don't trust Megan, but, well, what if the baby gets hungry while we're gone?''

"Give the breast pump a try and leave a bottle for Marie.'' Never in his life had Dan believed he would be telling a woman who was no relation to use a breast pump. Delivering a baby and then living with mother and baby for several weeks induced a level of intimacy he hadn't so far experienced with anyone else, not even Jean.

Bruce must think he was some kind of clod, warning him Fay was in no shape to have sex and wouldn't be for the length of time she stayed with him. He hoped to hell his brother hadn't thought sex was the reason he'd offered to have Fay stay at the cabin until she was strong enough to go home. Any man with a few brain cells wouldn't try seducing a woman who'd recently given birth. Which didn't mean he was never tempted.

Well, okay, so he was getting more tempted all the time, finding himself wanting to touch Fay. He'd touched her the night they saw the wolves, just a friendly arm over her shoulders. And what had that led to? He'd come damn close to kissing her.

"You're right," Fay said after a long silence. "I should at least test the breast pump. And I admit I'd enjoy getting out for a bit. It's a date."

"Our first night on the town."

She laughed. "It seems like ages since I was taken out to dinner, let alone a fish-fry. My dad used to take us to a lot of fish-frys when I was a kid. I can remember my mother muttering that broiling fish, like she did, was preferable. He always agreed, but we went anyway."

"Sounds like your folks had a good marriage."

"Oh, they did. While Mom was alive, my father wasn't such an old curmudgeon."

Dan couldn't help wondering once again, as all his siblings had, why their mother had left their dad without a word to any of them. He and Will had been in college by then, but it was still a shock. Somehow it made all his happy childhood memories seem false.

"Going back to our Friday night 'date,'" she said, "what was that about a picture window at the lodge?"

"It's a surprise for newcomers. You'll have to wait."

"I hate delayed surprises."

He grinned at her. "Tough."

That evening, as Dan was writing another list of supplies to pick up in town, Fay prowled around the cabin.

"I've been meaning to ask you what this old oak piece in the alcove is," she said.

He looked up. "An old wind-up phonograph."

"Good heavens, I've heard about them, but I've never seen one."

"Guess you're not an antique shopper then."

"No, not me. I like modern. How does it work?"

Dan crossed to where she stood beside his grandfather's—or maybe his great-grandfather's—phonograph. He opened the cabinet doors and showed her the albums of records stacked inside. Sliding one out at random, he lifted the lid and fit the record over the turntable. Then he spun the wind-up crank on the right side of the machine. When it felt tight, he placed the needle onto the record and turned the start lever.

"Paul Whiteman and his Cliquot Club Eskimos," he said as the music began to play.

Fay stared, fascinated, at the record spinning around. "It sounds so different." She bent and slid out another record. "These are heavy. Stiff, too. The song on this one is 'Sunny'."

"They're 78. State of the art at the time." He plucked the record from her fingers, set it aside and held out his hand. "Ms. Merriweather, may I have the pleasure of this dance?"

"You may, sir." She placed her hand in his.

After a moment he figured out the beat and, holding her lightly, danced across the cabin floor, passing the cradle where the baby slept, undisturbed by the music.

"What fun," Fay said. "I haven't danced for so long I'm surprised I can still remember how." When the record reached the end, she sighed. "They don't last long, do they?"

While he sorted through some of the stored records, she wound up the phonograph. "How about a waltz?" he asked.

"Smashing. That sounds like something they'd say in the old days. Or, maybe, the cat's pajamas."

He eased "The Blue Danube" onto the turntable and started the machine. As he put his arms around Fay, a fragment of memory surfaced. His mother was dancing with him as a teenager, saying, "Your father never would learn, but I intend to make sure all my sons know how to dance."

Then he forgot everything else but Fay. The music, even with the tinny sound of the orchestra on a phonograph from the old days, filled the room. Meanwhile her scent—clean, with a slight smell of roses—filled his head. Without thinking about it, he held her closer, whirling her about the room, the feel of her body against his warming him, heating him.

"A waltz is so romantic," Fay murmured. "Imagine that we're in a ballroom in Vienna in the old days. Instead of jeans, I'm wearing a beautiful gown and you're in one of those striking Austrian uniforms."

He glanced down at her face, nestled near his shoulder. She'd closed her eyes and he felt as though he could never let her go.

All too soon, the waltz ended. Before he could bring himself to release her, she opened her eyes, looked up at him and before he understood what he meant to do, he bent his head and kissed her.

Her lips were warm and responsive, inviting him to hold her closer, to deepen the kiss, but he struggled against the urge. This wasn't the time. When she finally pulled back, he reluctantly let her go and they stood for a moment gazing into each other's eyes.

"Is that the way a waltz is supposed to end?" she murmured.

"Certainly. After all, we were in old Vienna." It took effort to keep his tone light.

"But now we're back in today," she said, turning away and going to stand by the cradle with her back to him.

He knew she'd welcomed the kiss. Perhaps like him, she even wanted more. Which they both knew was impossible under the circumstances.

"I'd like to see you in a beautiful ball gown," he told her.

She turned toward him. "You've certainly never seen me at my best." She lifted a strand of her hair and let it fall. "Actually, you've never even seen me looking normal."

He told her the truth. "I like the way you look."

She rolled her eyes. "Thanks, but I really can't believe you. My hair is limp and badly needs styling, I may not be quite as pale as a ghost anymore, but I'm not really rosy-cheeked either. Besides, I can't even fit into my ordinary clothes yet."

Hearing the quiver in her voice on the last few words, he tried to think of something comforting to say, but all he could come up with was, "Will you believe me if I say I like you?"

She gave him a tremulous smile. "I guess I can go that far. I like you, too, Dan Sorenson."

"Glad to hear it." He crossed to her and held out his hand. "Being friends in today's world is a pretty good deal. Right?"

They shook hands. Though she had a firm grip, her hand still felt fragile in his.

The baby began to fuss and Fay picked her up. Without looking at him, she said, "Vienna was a fun place to visit, though."

As he watched Fay get ready to nurse Marie, he suddenly realized he didn't want to be an onlooker. The kiss had changed everything for him and he couldn't look at Fay's bared breast as she nursed the baby in the same way he had up until now. Damn, he hadn't counted on lust settling into the cabin with them, an unwelcome guest.

No more kisses, Sorenson, no more trips to old Vienna. We've got at least another week to get through together here. She's a friend. A woman who just delivered a baby and is nursing it. Lust is not the name of the game. Keep that in mind.

Chapter Six

The next morning, Fay woke to discover Dan wasn't in the cabin. Just as well, she wasn't quite sure she was ready to see him after what had happened last night. If only she hadn't responded to that kiss. She decided to get dressed so she'd be fully armed for the first meeting of the day and headed for the bathroom.

He still wasn't inside when she entered the kitchen, so she fixed herself a bowl of cereal and ate it. After checking that Danny Marie was still sleeping, she grabbed a jacket and stepped into the cool May morning. She heard the faint sound of gunshots. Okay, so he was target-practicing.

Another of her father's proclamations popped into her head. "Never get between a man and his gun." Okay, she'd stay put. She settled into one of the Adirondack chairs on the porch and waited for the gunshots to cease.

After a time she caught a flicker of red from the corner of her eye, turned her head and saw Dan emerging from the woods at the side of the cabin. He didn't look her way, so she got up and followed him around to the back, wanting to get this first post-kiss meeting over with.

He turned and saw her. "Eyes in the back of your head?" she called.

"A good cop always knows when he's being stalked," he called back.

"So now I'm stalking you?"

"Isn't that every man's wish? To be stalked by a beautiful woman?"

Even at her best, she wasn't sure "beautiful" applied to her, so she decided to ignore that. "Admit it, you heard me."

"Ears like a fox," he agreed.

"A fox?"

"Sure. They can hear mice run under the snow in the winter. That's how they catch their dinner."

"You're full of wilderness trivia. How's your marksmanship?"

"A bit off. Lack of practice'll do it every time."

Fay found herself unable to keep the conversation going. As an up-front type, she usually tried to bring up issues and resolve them, in relationships as well as business. But this wasn't exactly an issue—it was more that the relationship had taken a shift she hadn't anticipated. And she found she didn't want to confront that right now. Still, she'd managed this first meeting after last night without showing her unease. Or had she? Dan was eyeing her speculatively.

Though she wasn't cold, she hugged herself. "Cool morning, think I'll go in."

He fell into step beside her. "Peanut okay?"

"Sleeping." It occurred to her that he seemed a bit on edge, too.

He didn't say anything more. Silence is fine, she told herself. Silence is golden. But it increased her unease.

"You needn't think you can win every game," she found herself saying.

He frowned, making her realize her words had come out of nowhere.

Finally he grinned at her. "We're talking cards here?"

"Close, but no bulls-eye."

"Has to be Scrabble then," he said as they entered the cabin. "I suppose you expect to beat me?"

"What else?" And she would. In any case talking about playing a board game was a lot safer than bringing up what had happened last night, just as Scrabble was a lot safer than dancing.

In the afternoon, they took a walk in the woods again, Marie in her sling strapped to Dan. They walked, for the most part, in silence, until Dan suddenly halted. "Look," he whispered. About three feet ahead, a doe stood between two pines, ears twitching, staring at them. Finally, she whirled about and white tail high, bounded from sight.

Fay let her breath out in a sigh, feeling privileged to have gotten so close to a deer. "She was beautiful."

"Been a good year for the herd. Lots of forage so they all look healthy."

"But they had to weather that awful storm with no shelter. It makes me shudder to think of it."

"Deer are pretty well designed to survive any weather."

After that, their conversation died away again, and Fay wondered why. Usually they had lots to say to each other. Had the kiss they'd shared last night changed things between them that much? Maybe they were merely responding to the quiet under the trees, but she didn't think so.

No wonder in the 1800s mothers worried about their young daughters learning to waltz. There was something about the music and being in a man's arms that led to unintended kisses.

Yet Dan's kiss had certainly been intentional. As had her response. She'd wanted to kiss him. She shook her head. Here she was exaggerating what had simply been a spontaneous act. After all, Dan was an appealing man, no denying it, and the two of them *were* alone together in this isolated cabin except for Danny Marie. Unfortunately, a little baby made a poor chaperone. For heaven's sake, they didn't need a chaperone. She might be physically attracted to Dan, what healthy woman wouldn't be? And men tended to get the hots for any fairly suitable woman they spent much time alone with. But they both knew she wasn't capable of consummating anything right now. Fay sighed. It would be nice to be held and cuddled, though. Something most men usually didn't have a clue about. Ken had been particularly dense about that. Touching had meant sex to him. Period.

And now poor Ken was gone and she felt guilty because she didn't mourn him more, and she was already attracted to another man.

Enough. She half smiled, reminded of how the kids in her high school Spanish class had taken up the word for enough, going around shouting *"Basta!"* at each other. Well, *basta* it was. Taking a deep breath, she turned to Dan and said, "How long is this great weather going to last?"

He glanced up through the branches at the sky. "Starting to cloud over. Could rain. If I'd remembered batteries for the radio, we'd know."

Yes, he thought, *and if I'd remembered the blasted batteries, the radio would've been working last night and we'd never have turned on the phonograph. Which would have avoided that damn kiss. It changed everything.*

Fay wasn't her usual talkative self and what she did say sounded strained—like she was trying too hard to be casual.

Hell, he probably was making too much of what happened. It could be she was just tired. She hadn't been napping much lately.

"Let's head back to the cabin," he said.

"Already?"

"You need to rest."

She scowled at him. "I think I'm the best person to decide whether or not I need to sleep or not."

"We're heading back," he said in the no-argument voice he used when making arrests.

She muttered something under her breath, then didn't say another word to him all the way back.

"Look," he said, once they were back in the cabin. "I told you not long after we met you were safe with me. That hasn't changed. Won't change."

"I'm not worried about that," she snapped.

"Then what the hell is wrong?" Despite himself, his voice raised.

Before she answered, from inside the pouch he still wore, the baby began to whimper.

Dan scooped her up, cradled her in his arms and said softly, "Sorry, baby, didn't mean to scare you."

"I guess that means we can't have the knock-down, drag-out fight I'm spoiling for," Fay said.

He heard the humor in her tone and gave her a reluctant grin. "Nope. Doesn't do to scare the kidlings."

"Kidlings? Where did you dig up that word?"

"When we were little we always knew we'd gone too far when Grandma said, 'Now, now, kidlings.' She never called us that unless she was really annoyed."

Fay held out her arms and Dan handed over the baby, who immediately began looking for a nipple. They settled on the couch and Dan busied himself elsewhere.

Later, when he figured she was through nursing, he checked on them and found Fay had fallen asleep, the baby held in the crook of her arm that was next to the couch back. As gently as he could, Dan extracted Marie and hoisted her onto his shoulder in case she hadn't burped. Fay didn't rouse. Her shirt was open, revealing the breast where the baby had nursed. He didn't try to tackle the bra, but, for his own peace of mind, he needed to conceal her breast from his sight. As he reached down and draped the shirt over her breast, Fay's eyelids fluttered.

She didn't rouse and he eased away, carrying Marie with him until she rewarded him with a burp. Then he changed her diaper, wrapped her in a blanket and brought her outside with him. Settling into one of the old wooden chairs on the porch, he propped her on his knees so she could look up at him and began to talk softly to her, mostly nonsense.

"You look at me with those big blue eyes like you understand every word I'm saying," he told her.

She gurgled and the corners of her lips curled up into a smile. His heart turned to mush.

Soon her eyes drooped shut and he rocked her very gently up and down. It took him a few minutes to realize what he was half-crooning, half-singing to her: "Bye baby bunting, Daddy's gone a-hunting..."

It was the lullaby he remembered his mother singing to Megan when she was a baby.

He stopped abruptly. Lifting Marie into his arms, he carried her inside and laid her in the cradle. He hadn't let himself think about his mother in years, not until after he'd met Fay. His mother was better left tucked into a corner of his mind. And he was better off not singing lullabies to Marie where he called himself Daddy. He wasn't her father. In a matter of weeks, she and her mother would be out of his life for good.

Fay woke abruptly, alarmed. She'd been nursing the baby, where—? Seeing Marie asleep in the cradle, she frowned, trying to remember if she'd put her there. No, because if she had, she'd have fastened her bra and buttoned her shirt. That triggered a vague recollection of Dan's warm fingers lightly touching her bare skin. Warmth curled within her. But wait, didn't that memory belong to the night Dan had taken her in and buttoned her into his grandfather's pajama top? Still, he must have put Marie in the cradle.

Enough speculation. Sitting up, she put herself to order. Dan was nowhere in sight. Listening, she heard the sound of someone chopping wood outside. She nodded, glad he wasn't in reach because it gave her time to get over her annoyance at him being right about her needing a nap. Which was silly. Why was she angry with him? She really didn't have a good reason. If it was about their relationship changing, she was as much at fault as he.

Okay, so it had to be herself she was mad at. Any relationship with Dan other than friendship was doomed to go nowhere. Once she was back in Archer she would be going back to work, part-time at first, but eventually full-time. There was no time in her life to worry about developing a relationship with a man right now. Especially another man who lacked the ambition to get ahead in his career.

She suddenly remembered she'd had the fiasco with Ken. She certainly hadn't meant to hurt Ken, but there was no way she could have married him once she realized he had no ambition to advance in his career.

He'd called her cold-hearted. Clear-headed would have been more accurate. Just because she had a yen to be held and cuddled at the moment, and Dan was the only available male, didn't mean she needed to muddy the waters any further.

When Dan came in carrying a load of kindling, she smiled at him. "You were right. What a difference a nap makes. Thanks for rescuing Marie. That's the first time I've actually fallen asleep holding her."

"You had her safely up against the back of the couch. But she did appreciate me picking her up. I got two rewards. The first was a burp." He dumped the kindling in the wood-box before adding, "The other was a smile. And don't tell me it was just gas. I know a smile when I see one.''

"Oh, no," she wailed. "I missed her very first smile."

"Now that she knows how, it'll be your turn next."

Relieved that she'd been able to free herself of any anger toward Dan, she smiled at him and said, "I'll admit you deserved to be first. Any nonmedical man who can deliver a baby, learn to give her a bath without dropping her and also change a diaper without stabbing her with pins, certainly deserves that reward."

Later, as she helped him prepare supper, Fay was pleased to find their relationship easing back into a casual friendship mode. The way it should be. She'd make sure it didn't get dislodged again.

After supper and after Marie was settled for the night, Dan said, "Didn't you say something about a game earlier?

"Has to be Scrabble," Fay said. "I'm set on coming out on top."

"Variety's more fun."

She toyed with the notion that might be a double entendre and decided to ignore it, if it was. "I want to win again and I will. Tonight."

"You sound wired. Expecting to win a trophy?"

"Why not? Is there one?"

"I'll come up with something."

"In your double solitaire, luck counted," she said. "It may count a bit in Scrabble, too, but skill is what wins."

"You trying to psych me out?"

She smiled. "Why, not? All's fair in—war."

He chuckled. "Seems to me that's not quite the way the quote goes. And, hey, it's only a game."

"I always come through with what I promise. That makes for success."

Ignoring his frown, she picked her letters, only to find the best word she could spell was lover. She plunked her letters down.

Dan spelled desire. When their glances crossed he grinned at her.

The game went on, with them trading places back and forth as to who was ahead. But when he tallied the scores, hers was higher.

"I did it!" she cried, jumping to her feet. "I won."

"Just like you promised," he said as he rose from his chair. "You'll be happy to know I've come up with a reward."

When he came close, she threw her arms around Dan and hugged him.

He hugged her close. "To get your reward," he said into her ear, "you need to lie face-down on the couch."

Bemused by the shivery tickle from his warm breath against her ear, she pulled away from him and obeyed. "What now?" she asked.

"Shift over a little so I can sit beside you."

When she did, he eased down and she felt his hands rest in the hollow of her back. "You've won a first-class back rub."

"Are you a masseur as well as a cop?"

"Nope, but in college I dated a gal who was getting her degree in physical therapy, and I learned a few things from her."

While Fay was wondering exactly what, he added,

"Did you know a back rub has a different purpose than a massage?"

He ran his hands up her spine, his fingers gently gliding over her vertebrae. As he rubbed her shoulders and then began to slide a hand down each side of her body, he said, "A back rub is used to relax the patient. A massage might also do that, but the purpose is to tone the muscles. The back rub is more caressing."

Was it ever. She imagined the gal from his college days doing this to him and was surprised to feel resentment.

"Don't tense up," he told her. "Defeats the purpose."

Whatever he was doing felt incredibly good. She not only relaxed completely but felt that in a few minutes she was going to turn to warm Jell-O and flow off the couch into a puddle onto the floor. "Don't ever stop," she murmured.

"A man knows he's doing something right when he hears those words from a woman."

She smiled. Maybe this wasn't cuddling, but what he was doing ranked right up there with it. She'd underestimated Dan.

"If I win again, do I get another back rub?" she asked.

"We might try leg massage or—"

"Thanks, but I'd rather stick to the back," Fay said.

"You don't know what you're missing."

She began to imagine Dan's hand rubbing her toes, her ankles, his hands sliding up her calves, over her knees and along her thighs. Which was a mistake because the back rub hadn't triggered erotic feelings.

Not until now, when her imagination took hold. She became conscious of how his fingers grazed the side of her breasts each time he ran his hands down. And how those hands rested for a moment on the curve of her buttocks before his fingers began the climb up her spine.

In no time at all she'd managed to work herself into a state that could lead nowhere. Summoning up a smidgen of willpower, she said, "Thanks, Dan, but I think I'm relaxed enough."

He removed his hands, saying, "Was the reward worth the fight?"

"I consider it a prize worth winning." Which was the understatement of the year.

He rose from the couch and looked down at her. "This reward works both ways, you know. When I win next time, it'll be your turn to give me a back rub."

She turned over and sat up. "Fat chance you'll win."

His eyebrows climbed. "Afraid?"

She shook her head. "It's just as well you won't win, because I've never given a back rub to anyone in my life."

"No problem. I'm just the man to teach you."

There *was* a problem. She couldn't very well admit that she was wary of touching people, but touching him was different. She actually wanted to touch him, and that was scary.

Come on, girl, she admonished herself. *What's touching him through his clothes going to do to you? It's not as though your hands would be on his bare skin.*

Unfortunately the thought of skin-to-skin contact

created such a vivid image in her mind that she felt her face flush.

"Well?" he said.

"I suppose on the off chance you do win, I can learn. It's just that…"

"What?"

Okay, she might as well admit at least part of it. "I'm not fond of touching people."

"Even friends?"

"It's silly, I know. I figure maybe it's because my parents weren't touchers so as a kid I guess I didn't learn that some kinds of touching were all right."

"You can begin to practice with me. There's nothing frightening about rubbing a friend's back."

Deciding there was no way she could back out without sounding really weird, Fay took a deep breath. "Luckily you don't stand a chance of winning, Sergeant."

"Just watch me, lady."

She eyed him sternly. "I'm beginning to think your 'reward' was just a sneaky way to get me to give you a back rub."

He grinned at her. "You wouldn't believe me if I denied it. About touching, though—that hug you gave me doesn't count?"

"Hugs are different. If something really fantastic happens, I might hug the person next to me. It's spontaneous, not thought about."

"Most of us 'touchers' don't plan ahead. I've never once thought about whether or not I should slap a good buddy on the shoulder when I meet up with him."

"Well, I do think about things like that. I just can't help it. Maybe your parents were more intimate."

Dan frowned and stared off into space.

Belatedly she remembered him telling her that his mother had left his father for another man and she could have bitten her tongue. Since there was no way to apologize, she didn't attempt it. Instead, she changed the subject.

"Tomorrow's Friday night, fish-fry night, right?"

He nodded.

"Casual, I hope. I really didn't bring anything dressy with me." Since he still seemed distracted, she added, "I probably wouldn't fit into any if I had. What a bummer—anemic and still a few pounds too heavy."

That focused him. He gave her a quick once-over before saying, "You look fine to me."

"You keep telling me that, but you've only seen me pregnant and now. I used to be, well, svelte."

"There's a word I never cozied up to. Svelte always meant skinny to me."

"I wasn't skinny."

"If you say so."

"I wasn't. I can show you pictures—" She broke off, realizing those pictures were back home in Archer and he wasn't ever likely to see them. Shifting quickly, she said, "We really need to finish the film in that disposable camera. How many pictures are left?"

"Six. Since it's going to rain tomorrow, let's wait so Megan can take an indoor shot of the two of us together when we drop Marie off."

Maybe I should take Megan up on her offer, Fay thought, *and stay in town instead of coming back here. It might be better for all concerned.* Except she knew it wouldn't. Even if Dan stayed at the house, too, it wouldn't be the same. The cabin was like a second home to her. Actually it was the only home Danny Marie had ever known. Not that the baby cared where she was as long as Mama was nearby. But Mama cared. Perhaps more than she should.

Luckily Danny Marie was not yet a month old. Too young to miss Dan, the one she'd bestowed her first smile on. Because it wasn't likely they'd see Dan again once they were back in Archer. Even if he called, Fay wasn't sure she'd want to see him. A friend, yes, but they really had very little in common. She doubted he would be persistent if she was cool to him. Which, of course, she would be. He surely would understand why.

Dan strode to the cradle, and Fay realized with a start that the baby was whimpering. She'd gotten so engrossed in her return-to-Archer scenario she actually hadn't heard her daughter's complaint. She watched him cuddle the baby to him, murmuring to her as he carried her to the table for a diaper change, and all of a sudden her chest felt as though a large and heavy rock had taken up residence there, a feeling she knew was emotional rather than truly physical.

In a couple of weeks she'd be leaving. And, though she and Dan might share the same city, in a sense, once she left the cabin, she would be leaving him for good, too.

It scared her to realize how much that disturbed her.

Chapter Seven

Despite the rain on Friday, or maybe because of it, Fay really looked forward to dinner out. Casual, Dan had said, but she wanted to—well, dazzle him. Impossible, given the fact, that though she was feeling a good deal better, her before pregnancy clothes still didn't fit right.

Still, when she examined herself in the bathroom mirror, she wasn't too disappointed. The gold silk scoop neck shirt covered the fact that the black velveteen pants were maternity wear. Her face had certainly regained some color in the past week, and her careful application of makeup made her look more like the self she was used to. Though her hair still needed styling, she'd pulled some of it back with a gold ornament.

Not so bad, she told herself. Maybe not svelte, but good enough, considering what she had to work with.

When she emerged into the main room, she was rewarded by the obvious admiration in Dan's eyes.

He wore jeans, with a dark blue turtleneck shirt under his casual jacket and he nodded in approval, though she privately felt this guy would look good in anything he wore. Or nothing? Damn, where had that wayward thought come from?

"I'm expecting a lot from that picture window surprise of yours," she warned him.

The rain had drizzled off to a fine mist by the time they reached Megan's house in town. As Fay settled a sleeping Danny Marie into the crib, she had second thoughts. Maybe they should take the baby with them.

As though he'd read her mind, Dan said, "Don't worry. Megan will overwhelm Marie with care, not ignore her."

Realizing that sooner or later she had to leave her daughter in someone else's care, Fay nodded, telling herself if Megan did run into trouble she could always call Dr. Bruce. But she worried all the way to the lodge. *Stop that!* she warned herself. *How can you ever go back to work if you have this delusion that only you or Dan can take care of your baby properly?*

Once inside the log lodge, she looked around, hoping to distract herself. Rustic, deliberately so, but it worked. The building was snuggled under tall evergreens, a true wilderness restaurant if ever there was one.

The dining room, with knotty-pine paneling, was a fair size and already half-filled, though it was still early. Once they were seated near the back of the room, Dan ordered a beer, but Fay stuck with water since she was nursing.

True to what he'd told her, a large window dominated the back wall, where outdoor spotlights illuminated a woodsy scene with a clearing in its midst. She glanced at Dan, eyebrows raised.

"Not yet. Be patient," he advised.

The fish, when it arrived, was delicious. So were the French fries. She was nearly through with the meal when she noticed something moving outside the picture window. She saw a man dump something in the middle of the clearing, then hurry out of sight. Certainly that couldn't be the surprise. She swallowed the last of the milk she'd ordered with the meal and almost choked when something huge and black ambled out of the pines toward the lodge.

"A bear," she muttered when she could speak. "That's a bear." She'd never seen one outside of a zoo.

Dan nodded.

"Is he tame?" she asked as the bear, looking impossibly large and cuddly at the same time, stopped in the middle of the clear space and began eating what had been dumped there.

"No, he's a wild bear. The lodge has a contract with him. They feed him leftovers every night in the same place and, in turn, he leaves their Dumpsters alone."

She blinked at him, half taken in, before she shook her head. "Come on."

"Okay, they lock their Dumpsters so they're bearproof. But he's learned to show up at the same time every night and not come around at any other time. The owner calls it operant conditioning. Bears rate high on the intelligence scale."

Watching the bear fascinated her, as it did the other

diners. He paid no attention to anything else but the food.

"I like your surprise," she told Dan.

They were getting ready to leave when a blond woman about Fay's age came up to their table. "Dan!" she exclaimed, giving him a hug. "It's been ages since I've seen you. Why didn't you tell me you were in town?"

"Actually I'm not, Anita," he said as he smiled down at the woman, who looked impossibly sexy in a tight red dress with heels to match.

"Oh?" Anita said.

"Good to see you," he told her.

Anita frowned as he placed a hand at the small of Fay's back and began to usher her out.

"Old girlfriend?" Fay asked when they reached his truck.

He shrugged. "I went to school with her."

Which told Fay exactly nothing. Since it was none of her business, what did it matter?

When they arrived to collect Danny Marie, Megan assured Fay the baby had been fine. "She didn't like the nipple on the bottle at first, but she got used to it fast," Megan said. "What a cutie."

Though she urged them to stay for coffee, Dan refused. "This is Fay's first night out. Let's not overdo it."

Fay waited until they got back in the truck with the baby before she said, "I can turn down my own invitations."

"What? Did you want coffee?"

She sighed. "No, but you refused for both of us without asking me—or even glancing toward me."

"I thought you'd be tired."

"If I am, that's beside the point. I could have made my own refusal, if you'd given me a chance."

He shrugged. "I figured if you wanted to stay you'd have said so."

So she could have. But he'd reminded her of how Ken used to make decisions without consulting her. Another reason their marriage wouldn't have worked. What was it with men?

They were almost back to the cabin before Fay remembered her manners. "I enjoyed my night out," she told Dan. "Thanks for the meal and the surprise."

"I hoped you would," he said. "Being confined to the cabin must be hard on a gal like you."

She took his words to bed with her, wondering if he had any idea how she really felt. But how could he, when even she wasn't sure herself?

The following afternoon, after the rain had become a half-hearted drizzle, Megan arrived for supper, bringing vegetable pasties with her and cookies for dessert.

"You realize you're our first dinner guest," Dan said as they sat down at the table.

"Should I feel honored?" Megan asked.

"Anyone who comes bearing the meal is always welcome," he teased.

"I hope you like carrots and rutabaga in your pasties along with the meat, potatoes and onions," Megan said to Fay.

"I'm not sure I've had rutabaga before," Fay said, "but they're delicious."

The meal passed pleasantly enough, but Megan had to leave almost immediately after. "Sorry to stick you with the dishes, but there's a meeting tonight I don't want to miss. The town is trying to build an animal shelter and some people are opposed to the idea. Can you imagine? They'll be there in force, but so will the good guys, meaning those for it, including me.''

''Try not to offer to be a pet foster parent,'' Dan said.

Megan gave him a withering look. ''He's never let me forget how many stray animals I brought home as a kid,'' she told Fay.

''Once even a goat,'' he put in. ''It climbed on to the shed roof, and Dad fell off the ladder trying to get it down. We all learned a few new words that day.''

After Megan left, and the dishes were cleared away and washed, Dan asked, ''Feel up to a Scrabble game?''

''If you mean am I tired, no. Or do you mean do I dare take the chance I'll have to give you a back rub?''

''I know you're a risk-taker.''

''No risk. I'll win. Again.''

The first letters she drew spelled out Anita, which, of course, she couldn't use. Adding another letter, she put in ''attain,'' but, as she did, to her dismay she found herself saying, ''Anita's quite pretty. She must have been popular in school.''

Dan stared at her for a moment as if asking what Anita had to do with anything, finally saying, ''She was Prom Queen her last year in high school.''

''I suppose you were Prom King.''

''Actually my brother Will was. I was still a sophomore.'' As he spoke, using one of her letters, he spelled out jealous. ''Got the *J* on a double space,'' he crowed.

She eyed him narrowly. Did he mean anything by that word he'd made?

"That'll put me way ahead," he added.

Apparently he didn't. But was she jealous? Is that why she'd persisted in asking him about Anita? Fay shook her head. If anything, it was probably because seeing Anita had reminded her that she had a ways to go yet before she'd look sexy again. Envy, possibly, but not jealousy.

She stopped thinking about it and concentrated on winning the game.

But she must not have concentrated hard enough, because when the scores were tallied, she'd lost by five points.

Dan grinned at her, rose, crossed to the couch and arranged himself face-down.

She sighed, made her way over and tried to sit next to him, but there wasn't room.

"You're too big," she told him.

"We'll have to use the loft."

Curiosity had driven Fay up the steps once when Dan was outside, so she knew that, besides the double bed, the room held a bureau, bedside table and a cedar chest. The decor was masculine stark. Apparently Dan's mother hadn't had a say in decorating the cabin.

This time, as she climbed the stairs to the loft behind Dan, she wasn't sure she liked the idea of going into his bedroom. She felt the couch was her turf, but the loft was Dan's.

No matter, she told herself. *I'm the one giving the back rub, the one in charge.*

She came to the top step and saw Dan already

sprawled on the bed, his T-shirt off. "You could have kept your shirt on," she complained. "I did."

"I didn't mention it last night, but the patient's back is supposed to be bare. Just thought I'd let you do it the right way."

"Gee, thanks, Sergeant." She sat down next to him and eyed his bare back.

After a moment of hesitation, she placed her hands on the small of his back, immediately feeling the warmth of his skin. When she eased her way up his spine to his neck, then down his shoulders and along his sides, she realized the procedure was more intimate than she'd figured. How did therapists distance themselves from their patients?

Still, if Dan hadn't been the person she was touching, she doubted she'd experience such intimacy. Under the superficial softness of his skin, she could feel the hard muscles of his back and, though she willed herself not to react, she was aware her pulse had quickened.

Think of it as a therapeutic procedure, she scolded herself, not foreplay.

"I'd be happy to have you go on forever," he murmured.

"Then I must be doing something right." She made her tone deliberately tart.

"Mmmm."

She half smiled, recognizing the sound as close to a purr. Obviously he was getting the same pleasure from her hands as she'd had from his.

Though she owed him as much time as he'd given her, how could she keep going and prevent herself from letting her hand drift over the curve of his butt? That would never do. Not at all.

Before she lost her cool completely, she felt a twinge in her shoulders. Relieved she could grab a real excuse, she said, ''I'm getting a little tired, so I guess this is as long as forever lasts.''

He sighed but didn't move. ''Go down and rest,'' he told her. ''I'll join you in a bit.''

Dan waited until he heard her on the stairs before he turned over and sat up, shifting uncomfortably. His own damn fault for allowing her to give him the back rub. It'd been bad enough when he had rubbed her back, what had he expected other than a complete arousal when he felt her hands stroking the bare skin of his back? In his bed, of all places. Hadn't his brother warned him to keep away from her?

Since there didn't seem to be any way he could touch her and not get aroused, he'd be a damn fool if he kept this up. More daytime walks in the woods, less—no, make that zero—evening touching. Hugs were out, too. Hell, he didn't even dare hold hands with her.

The weather turned sunny once more, gradually warming as the days passed. After the tow truck Dan had arranged for came and hauled the wrecked rental car away, for some reason, the time seemed to speed by to Fay. She was caught by surprise when Dan announced that this was the day Bruce had scheduled to see her again.

''Already?'' she said, the word escaping before she thought.

''Haven't you looked in the mirror lately?''

She'd known, while refusing to think about how it meant an end to her time with Dan, that she was much stronger and the color had returned to her face. Examining her fingernails, she noted their unmistakable pinkness. Which meant her count must be getting back to normal. If that proved true, it would be time for her to go home.

Home. Not this cabin, but to her apartment in Archer. A lovely and desirable apartment, in one of the town's big old houses. Her widowed landlady, Clara Monroe, who lived in the rest of the house, was a descendant of the original builder. Fay loved her apartment and was fond of Clara. Yet the thought of leaving Dan depressed her.

"You're quiet today," he said as they drove into town.

She couldn't tell him the truth. Instead, she said, "You never told me when the rental company would have another car ready or how I'm supposed to get it."

"That's because you won't need it."

She stared at him. "What do you mean? I'm sure your brother is going to tell me I'm well enough to go home. How do you expect me to get there?"

"In my truck. I'm driving you back to Archer."

"But—but have they called you back to duty?"

He shrugged. "They'll find some desk job to keep me off the streets until the board wraps things up. It should be soon. There's no reason you should push your luck by driving all that way downstate with the baby when I have to go to the very same town." His glance at her clearly said *argue if you dare.*

She decided not to, admitting to herself she was relieved by his offer.

At Dr. Bruce's office, Fay's prediction proved true. "I'm pleased with how well you're doing," he told her. "Your count is borderline normal now, so there's no reason you can't return home. If you'll sign a release form and give me the name and address of your doctors in Archer, I'll send them my records for both you and your daughter. It's important you make an appointment with your doctor as soon as possible. You need to discuss with him such things as how long you plan to nurse the baby and he can advise you about when it's safe to resume sex.''

''I'll do that,'' she promised, hoping he wouldn't notice her flush. For some reason Bruce's mention of sex unsettled her, though it hadn't when she'd discussed it with her doctor back home. Perhaps it was because Bruce was Dan's brother.

''Dan's driving you and the baby back to Archer, I understand,'' he said.

She nodded, wondering if he disapproved.

''Probably a good idea, since the baby's so young. Driving alone with an infant can be distracting. She's gained weight by the way—a healthy little girl.''

''Thanks for all you've done for me. I really appreciate it.''

He smiled, looking for a moment remarkably like Dan. ''I told my brother that he did so well with your delivery he ought to reconsider and go into medicine. He said the day I joined the police force he'd think about it.''

She smiled now. ''Somehow I can't visualize you as a cop.''

''Neither can I. To each his own.''

''Dan saved my life,'' she said. ''My daughter's, too. I can never repay him.''

Bruce gave her a look she couldn't interpret. ''You don't need to try.''

It almost sounded like a warning and she was still

thinking about what Bruce could have meant as she and Dan drove over to say goodbye to Megan.

"I just put new film in my camera," Megan said. "Let me take a farewell picture of you two with the baby. I can't get over how much she's grown."

Later, as they were leaving, Megan hugged Marie and Fay, and lastly Dan. "Don't bother cleaning up the cabin," she said as she let him go. "I'll use my key and take care of all that this weekend."

Fay was about to protest that they could at least start the process, when Dan shook his head at her. So she simply thanked Megan.

Back in the truck, Dan said, "When Megan offers to clean up there's no use arguing. She's been trying to mother all of us since—well, for a long time now. She gets upset if you don't let her."

Since their mother left? Is that what Dan meant? Fay sighed. Poor Megan, feeling she needed to try to act as a substitute when, after all, she must have missed her mother as much or more than any of them, being the youngest and the only girl.

"Need anything from the general store?" Dan asked. "I have to stop there a minute."

She didn't and they were soon on their way again. Tonight, she thought, is the last night we'll spend together. "It's time to take up my life again," she said, more to herself than to Dan.

He didn't reply, but she hadn't expected him to.

"In a way, being in the cabin has been like living in another world," she went on. "A fantasy world."

After a silence, he said, "Sometimes I think the entire Upper Peninsula is another world."

"That, too, but…" She didn't go on, unsure she could find words to express how she felt. Taking a deep breath, she said, "I'm looking forward to getting back to work."

He glanced at her. "Who'll take care of Peanut?"

"My landlady, Mrs. Monroe. She offered to when I was pregnant."

"How old is she? Can she cope with a small baby?"

How dare he question her judgment? Then she reminded herself how fond he was of her daughter and tamped down her annoyance. "Clara Monroe raised three children of her own successfully. As for her age, she's sixty-five and full of energy."

Dan grunted, but said nothing more.

They reheated refrigerator leftovers for supper. Afterward Fay nursed her daughter and got her ready for the night. As usual, Dan didn't so much as glance her way as she nursed, but she no longer commented on it, aware that ever since the night they'd waltzed together, there'd been a certain tension between them. Not that they'd stopped being friends, but a new dimension had been added. Other than the reward back rubs, he almost never touched her. Nor she, him. It was safer that way, but that didn't stop her from regretting that they had to play it so safe.

Once Danny Marie was asleep in the cradle, Fay looked around for Dan, finding him nowhere in the house. Restless, she pulled on a sweater and went out to the porch. Though it wasn't warm enough to leave the door open, the late May night was mild. She stood on the porch looking up at the moon, waning from full, as it rose over the pines. Words from an old country song came to mind, something about the moon looking lonesome shining through the trees.

Lonesome wasn't a word that applied to her time here at the cabin and yet tonight maybe it did. Without conscious thought, she began to hum the song, a few more of the words coming back to her. Like a lot of country songs, it was a plaintive tale of a lover leaving.

She was leaving. But Dan wasn't and never would be her lover. And, actually, he was going with her. They both were leaving.

A faint fragrance drifted through the night air, reminding her of the tiny pink flowers Dan had shown her on one of their walks through the woods.

"Trailing arbutus," he'd told her. "Nothing else smells quite as sweet."

No more walks in the woods with Dan. Nothing else would ever be quite like those walks.

A dark figure stepped from between the trees. The moonlight told her it was Dan. In silence, she watched him walk toward the porch, watched him climb the few steps, all the time thinking this would be the last time she'd stand at the railing and watch him. But she didn't move or speak.

He came up behind her, so close she could feel his breath stir a strand of her hair. Close but not quite touching. She wanted to be touched. Needed to be touched.

One last time. She deliberately took a step backward. When she felt his arms go around her waist, she closed her eyes, savoring the feel of his body against hers.

For a long time neither of them spoke.

"You called this a fantasy world," he murmured at last. "Tonight it seems like one."

She sighed. "Fantasies aren't real. This world isn't real."

"You feel real enough to me."

She struggled against her urge to turn in his arms so she was facing him, wanting his lips on hers, wanting—him. At the moment nothing else mattered.

From the woods, an owl hooted four times, its mournful cry bringing her back to what was possible and what wasn't. Deliberately focusing on the owl, she said, "Why do they always hoot four times?"

"They don't. Sometimes it's three."

She recognized the hoarseness in his voice for what it was—need. Not that she already wasn't aware of his arousal pressing against her back. If she didn't move away from him the fantasy might overwhelm them both.

"I wish..." she murmured, not specifying what.

"So do I." He whispered the words into her ear, making her melt against him.

Still holding her, he stepped backward, bringing her with him. A moment later, his hands moved up to her shoulders, he turned her sideways and then eased her down into one of the porch chairs. He sat in the one next to her.

The decision made, she did her best to accept it. It was, after all, the only choice. "Moonlight is as dangerous as a waltz," she said.

He didn't comment. Would he, she wondered, talk about seeing her once they were back in Archer? She'd already made up her mind that wouldn't work out. Part of the desire they both felt, she was sure, was because of where they were—alone together in a wilderness cabin under most unusual circumstances.

When the silence continued, she said, "Tomorrow

we go our separate ways.'' Though she'd striven for a light tone, to her own ears her voice sounded plaintive. Hurriedly, she added, ''Back to the real world.''

''It's too bad you have to go to work so soon,'' he said.

She looked at him, but he was staring into the darkness between the trees. ''Why wouldn't I?'' she asked.

''So you could be with Marie more. She's so little.''

''I'm starting out part-time.''

''Still…''

She shifted in her chair, turning so she faced him. ''When you run a private consulting business, you can't afford to let your clients forget you.''

He glanced at her. ''I'm not arguing the point.''

''Then what *are* you doing?''

''Babies need their mothers.''

Her annoyance dribbled into her words. ''Don't you think I know that? I plan to spend as much time as I can with my daughter. At the same time I'm a single parent and I can't let my business falter.''

When he didn't reply, still miffed at him, she said, ''Sometimes you remind me of my father.'' As soon as the words were out of her mouth she regretted them.

Dan turned to look at her. ''Your father?'' His voice was even, but she sensed anger simmering underneath.

''Not really,'' she admitted. ''I suppose I was annoyed because you're ignoring the basics of my situation. I'm the one who'll be supporting my child. To support her I need to work. If I don't start soon, my clients will forget me and I can't afford to let that happen since a lot of my business comes from word of mouth. Remember, I don't work for a company, so I don't get a steady paycheck.''

"I hadn't forgotten that you're a high-powered freelance consultant.''

The way he said it ruffled her feathers, making her next words angry rather than reasoned. "The truth is *some* of us realize it's important to rise as high as we can.''

After a moment, he said, in an icy voice, "Others of us understand the importance of knowing when we've reached the place we want to be.''

"Like my father?'' she retorted.

"So now we're back to how like your father I am?''

He was impossible. "I think it's time we both went to bed,'' she snapped. "Separately.''

"What else?'' He rose and strode off into the moonlight, leaving her alone on the porch.

She watched until he disappeared into the darkness before getting up and going into the house. What an infuriating man. He'd not only walked off on her, but left having had the last word.

She made sure the baby was all right, then put on her nightgown and curled on the couch under her quilt. She certainly didn't care to come face-to-face with Dan again tonight. All she'd really meant was that she could imagine her father complaining about her going to work and leaving the baby with a care-taker—the baby he hadn't wanted her to have in the first place.

Naturally she couldn't fall asleep, but she kept her eyes closed when she heard Dan come in the back door, doing her best to breathe slowly and evenly. She thought he paused by the couch, but she wasn't sure. Then she heard him climbing the stairs to the loft. Where he'd be getting into the bed where she'd given him a back rub. And here she was lying on the sofa, where he'd given her a back rub.

Just as well they were leaving the cabin in the morning. There were too many memories here, memories she had to lose.

Back in Archer there would be none.

When he came downstairs in the morning, Dan hoped Fay would be herself and not spout a lot of superficial conversation neither of them wanted to hear. Silence he wouldn't mind, but false cheerfulness after a night of too little sleep was sure to put him even more on edge.

As he made the coffee, bits and pieces of last night played back in his mind. Like her father, was he? What the hell kind of statement was that? He might not want children of his own, but he'd never advise anyone who was already pregnant to get rid of a baby. What a woman decided to do was up to each individual and, as far as he was concerned, if a man wasn't the father of the child in question he should keep his mouth shut.

Dan didn't think he'd get along with Fay's father. Not that he figured he'd ever meet him.

He knew from what she'd said about the cabin that she must have mixed feelings about leaving. He damn well did. She'd been right about them needing to return to the real world, though. And none too soon. A clean break was best. He never would marry again and he was none too sure he'd even like the high-powered Archer Fay. As for Marie...

A muscle twitched in his jaw. He didn't want to think about not seeing the little girl again. Megan had said yesterday that it was strange how quickly a baby could work her way into your heart. He shrugged. Instinct. Must have to do with why the human race had survived.

"Do I smell coffee?" Fay's sleepy voice asked.

He glanced toward the couch and saw her sitting up, hair tousled, the pink back in her cheeks. She looked infinitely desirable. "Thought I'd finish up the eggs by making cheese omelets," he said, turning from her.

"Sounds good," she told him. "I'll get dressed and help."

So far she sounded matter-of-fact. Which suited him. Could be she was as relieved as he that this sojourn was at an end.

At breakfast they had little to say to each other. What was there left to say? Afterward, she fed the baby while he cleaned up the kitchen. Then it was time to finish whatever packing hadn't been done and load the truck. When he had his gear in, he picked up the cradle and started out with it.

"Are we stopping by Megan's again to drop off the cradle?" Fay asked.

He shook his head. "I cleared it with Bruce and Megan already. They both want you to keep the cradle."

She stared at him. "But—but it's a Sorenson family heirloom."

"We'd like you to have it."

"What a wonderful gift. I'll treasure it." She turned her face away, but not before he saw tears in her eyes.

With the truck loaded, Marie bundled into her car bed and Fay buckled into the front seat, Dan took a minute to look around, taking a deep breath of the pine-scented air before climbing into the pickup.

"We're off," he said as he maneuvered the truck along the narrow drive.

Fay said nothing until they were almost in Evergreen Bluff, which they had to go through on their way. "The photos," she said. "We forgot to pick them up."

"Did that yesterday. I stuffed them in the glove compartment."

"Without looking at them?"

"Guilty as charged." No way was he going to tell her he was in no mood for reminders yesterday. Or today, for that matter. That's what photos were—reminders.

She pulled out the envelope and opened it. "Two sets," she said. "So we can each have one."

Great. Just what he didn't need. He would send his set to Megan.

At first Fay's comments ranged from, "Isn't she cute?" to "You look positively grim in this one." Then she stopped talking and, he saw she was sorting them into two stacks, her expression sad.

He turned on the radio.

"Must we listen to country music?" she snapped.

Since he wasn't a great fan himself, he flicked it off.

"I put your set back in the envelope," she said. "Remember it's in the glove compartment again."

"Yo."

"There's a word I've always hated."

She hated yo? "You sound a bit testy."

"You'd be that way, too, if you didn't get a decent night's sleep. That whippoorwill started up sometime after midnight and I thought he'd never stop."

"I heard him."

"So you know what a pest he was."

He'd heard the bird because he was already awake. Or still awake.

Long before they reached the Mackinac Bridge, Fay fell asleep. She didn't rouse until the baby woke up just below the Straits. He pulled over and parked in a rest area so Fay could nurse the baby. He got out to stretch his legs while she did.

When they resumed driving, Fay turned on the radio and found a station playing jazz. "Do you mind?"

He could take or leave jazz, so he shrugged. Under the circumstances, he preferred any kind of music to conversation.

By the time they reached Archer, he felt so morose he didn't trust himself to say anything. Fay directed him to her apartment and, while she carried the baby in, he unloaded the cradle and her belongings, bringing them into her apartment. On one of his trips back and forth, he met the landlady.

"Mr. Sorenson is a friend of mine," Fay told Mrs. Monroe.

He muttered a polite greeting to the gray-haired woman and went back for the last item, the car bed.

The landlady was bending over the cradle, cooing, when he returned. He quelled the need he felt to hold the baby one last time and turned to Fay. He managed to say "Goodbye," despite the tightness that threatened to shut down his throat.

She looked up at him, her hazel eyes unreadable.

Because the urge to gather her up and hold her to him was almost unbearable, he turned and, without another word, walked out of her apartment and, he figured, her life.

Chapter Eight

Because she hadn't slept much the night before, Fay fell asleep early in her own bed in her own apartment in Archer. She woke hearing Danny Marie's hungry wails from the cradle she'd placed beside her bed. There was a brand-new crib in the second bedroom, along with the other baby paraphernalia, but she'd wanted her daughter close to her. She lifted the baby from the cradle and carried her into the nursery, where the changing table, diapers and a comfortable rocker waited.

After Danny Marie once more wore clean diapers, Fay settled into the rocking chair with her to nurse. "We're alone, little one," she murmured. "Just you and me, the way it's supposed to be."

Peanut, Dan called the baby. No, she wasn't going to start reminiscing. The time in the cabin was over. Done with. He obviously felt the same way, his abrupt goodbye was proof of that. Couldn't wait to get rid of them both. Not that continuing the relationship would have worked anyway. Hadn't she rejected the idea even before she got back here? Why should she feel hurt because he'd come to the same conclusion?

When Danny Marie finished nursing, Fay burped her, then held her so she could look into her daughter's face. Blue eyes gazed back at her. Not Dan's eyes, of course, but close to the same color. Fay sighed. So she missed him. In no time at all she'd get used to being on her own again. She'd never minded it before, had enjoyed the privacy, in fact.

Privacy was something she cherished. After they became engaged, Ken had wanted her to move in to his condo with him. She'd refused, even though he'd pointed out she'd be doing that after they married. In fact, the argument had been part of what had made her rethink the entire idea of marriage. That and the sudden emergence of Ken's jealousy. Naturally she sometimes had lunch with clients when she was out of town, it was part of the package and often the best time to discuss any problem that had arisen.

Since Ken also worked out of town for his firm, he knew about business lunches. Why he'd suddenly decided to equate her business lunches with her cheating on him was beyond her comprehension. Until one of her friends pointed out that maybe he was using his business lunches to cheat on her and figured she must be doing the same thing. Though she'd never confronted him about that, it wasn't long before she backed out of the marriage and the relationship.

She sighed. While those had been contributing factors, what really made her change her mind was the realization that she didn't love Ken. She remembered telling Dan how guilty she'd felt when Ken died. Dan had held her while she cried, saying it hadn't been her fault and, somehow, had made her feel better.

Just the same, it was a shame Ken would never know he had a daughter. On the other hand, he'd never indicated he'd wanted children. Had he? She'd never know. Dan didn't, he'd made no bones about that.

"It's really strange," she told her daughter, "how I wind up thinking about Dan no matter what's on my mind to begin with."

Danny Marie smiled at her.

Fay smiled, too, wondering if the baby missed Dan as much as she did. She shook her head. Danny Marie was far too young to remember him.

Everything fades with time, Fay assured herself. *Eventually I won't remember, either. It's not as though Dan and I were lovers. What we had in common was enforced intimacy, because he had to deliver my baby and then take care of both of us.*

Over the next few days, while she tried to decide which of her regular clients to approach first, she kept expecting Dan to call, just to ask how things were going. Wasn't it common courtesy? When he didn't, she felt angry that he'd been able so easily to put their shared time in the cabin behind him. Why should she be missing him when it was obvious he didn't care enough to even ask after the baby?

If all she could do was stew over the past, it definitely was time for her to start her consulting work again. On an impulse, she called the business owner she'd had to turn down during the last month of her

pregnancy because the job he'd wanted done would
have taken months rather than weeks to finish. If he
still wanted her, her commute wouldn't be far. An
ideal situation.

"Congratulations on the baby girl," he said. "No,
I haven't yet found anyone with your qualifications—
or your reputation for getting things done and done
right. I'm delighted you called. The job's yours."

"See," she told Danny Marie after she hung up,
"your mommy's still *numero uno.*"

Fay then called Clara Monroe to make baby-sitting
arrangements.

"I've been dying to get my hands on that cute little
girl of yours," Clara told her. "My grandkids are
both long past the baby stage and I miss that. Bring
her over and we'll have pie and coffee while we discuss how this is going to work out."

But, even though Fay trusted Clara implicitly,
when she set off two mornings later to drive to work
in a nearby city, she worried. She'd left three bottles
of breast milk in the refrigerator, so that was no problem, but what if Danny Marie suddenly got sick?

Clara had the number of the baby's pediatrician and
she'd weathered illness in her own kids and grandkids.

Still, what if Danny Marie sensed a stranger taking
care of her and got upset?

Unlikely. The baby had taken to Clara from the
first.

What if—?

Stop it! she admonished herself. *You know Clara
is a loving, responsible person. Nothing is going to
go wrong. Danny Marie will get along just fine.*

Eventually she arrived at work and started in on

the project needing completion. The immediate problems she spotted focused her mind on what she was doing rather than worrying about her daughter.

The next time she went in it was easier to leave the baby with Clara, but, as the days passed, Fay found what she was doing at work was not as all-consuming to her as it once had been. She missed being with her baby.

"Mommy has to work sometimes," she told Danny Marie on the weekend when she took her in the carrier pouch to the park several blocks from the apartment. "Work means we pay the rent."

Though the park wasn't a woods, it was dotted with big old maples and an oak or two. The remains of daffodils and tulips added splashes of color. No piney smell, but the scent of lilacs sweetened the air. A squirrel scampered across the sidewalk in front of her and ran up an oak. "See, even wildlife," Fay said as much to herself as to the baby.

The park reminded her of the one on the other side of town where her father used to take her when she was little. She remembered how she liked him to push her on the swing, higher and higher—way up past where her mother would ever push her. She'd never been a timid child.

Which brought her to that message on her answering machine that she'd not yet acknowledged. While she was away, her father had called to ask if she was okay. She'd left Aunt Marie's number on her recorded message, so he had to know where she'd gone. Except she hadn't gone there, had she? But she was almost positive he wouldn't have bothered to call her aunt, so he would assume she was in Duluth. No need to call him back. She wasn't ready to. Maybe she never would be.

And she certainly had no intention of ever getting in touch with Dan, who hadn't left any messages.

Ten days at work and Dan was slowly going nuts. The chief had told him privately that the board decision was positive and would be official by Monday. He sure as hell hoped so. He'd never liked being tied to a desk. Which wasn't the entire problem. Maybe if he'd been busier he wouldn't be thinking about Fay and the baby so much. He'd had no clue they would be constantly on his mind. He worried as much about them as if they were family.

There wasn't a damn thing he could do about it. No point in calling when she'd made it clear that she wouldn't want to hear from him. What Fay needed, whether she realized it or not, was a marriage-minded man who'd take care of her and Marie. But he definitely was not that man, which he knew and so did Fay.

Okay, Sorenson, you want to make your move on a gal who needs you like she needs major surgery? Forget it, man.

The trouble was he couldn't. Not until Monday, when the paperwork to put him back on full duty came through. He immediately immersed himself in a case that'd been hanging fire. He'd made some notes on the case before he got shot, but he was damned if he could find them.

By Wednesday, after looking over the office, the car he used for work and the apartment for a small notebook he'd made the notes in, he finally remembered what he'd done with it. He'd shoved the notebook in the glove compartment of the pickup before he drove to the U.P. After he got off work, he went to retrieve it. The notebook was there all right, but, while pulling it out, he knocked an envelope with the photos onto the floor. When he picked it up, some of the photos slid out. Fay's smiling face stared up at him.

Muttering a curse, he grabbed photos and notebook and slammed into the apartment. He fully intended to shove the photos in a drawer and be done with it, but, instead, he found himself at the kitchen table, spreading them out almost like a solitaire game.

He found the snapshot where Fay had claimed he looked grim. She'd been right. But the ones he looked at again and again were those of Fay. And the baby. He sighed, shrugged and picked up his cell phone.

Mrs. Monroe answered. "Oh, I remember you," she said. "You're the one who drove Fay home. But she's not back from work yet, though she should be at any moment. Wait, I think I hear her at the door now."

After a few minutes, Fay came on the phone. "Dan?" she said.

"Thought I'd call to see how things were going," he said. "I hear you've gone back to work."

"You don't sound any too thrilled about it," she said.

He'd heard the gruffness in his own voice, so he couldn't very well deny it. "I'm not. Even though it's none of my business."

"I'm sure you know how the world turns," she said tartly. "No work, no pay. Besides I was getting restless."

"How's the baby?"

"Getting along just fine with Clara." Her tone told him he'd riled her. Which he hadn't meant to do.

"The weather's been good," he said.

"You called to discuss the weather?"

"If the weather isn't good, how can you have a picnic?"

"A picnic?"

"Yeah, like in a park or somewhere. I thought it'd be something the baby would enjoy." He hadn't planned to ask her to go anywhere when he made the call, but the words just came tumbling out.

"Da—that is, Marie is too young to notice."

"Wrong. Babies are busy processing the world in their first few months."

"I'd hate to deprive her." Her tone held a trace of amusement mixed in with the tartness.

"So?"

"At the moment I work Mondays, Wednesdays and Fridays. Tuesdays and Thursdays are pretty much needed catch-up days."

No mention of weekends. Which meant she was considering it. "How about Sunday?"

"Sunday?" she repeated. In the background he could hear Clara Monroe say something.

"Not so good," Fay said. "Clara says it's supposed to rain on Sunday."

Damn. He should have checked the weather. Would have if he'd had any idea he was going to invite her on a picnic of all things. Chances are he'd wind up working part of Saturday, but he wasn't going to give up. "Saturday, then. If I get called in, I'll let you know."

"I wouldn't want to interfere with—"

The Silhouette Reader Service™—Here's How It Works:

Accepting your 2 free books and gift places you under no obligation to buy anything. You may keep the books and gift and return the shipping statement marked "cancel." If you do not cancel, about a month later we'll send you 6 additional books and bill you just $3.99 each in the U.S., or $4.74 each in Canada, plus 25¢ shipping & handling per book and applicable taxes if any.* That's the complete price and — compared to cover prices of $4.75 each in the U.S. and $5.75 each in Canada — it's quite a bargain! You may cancel at any time, but if you choose to continue, every month we'll send you 6 more books, which you may either purchase at the discount price or return to us and cancel your subscription.

*Terms and prices subject to change without notice. Sales tax applicable in N.Y. Canadian residents will be charged applicable provincial taxes and GST.

OFFICIAL OPINION POLL

ANSWER 3 QUESTIONS AND WE'LL SEND YOU
2 FREE BOOKS AND A FREE GIFT!

0074823 ‖‖█‖█‖█‖‖ ‖‖█‖‖‖ ‖‖█‖‖‖   **FREE GIFT CLAIM #** 3953

YOUR OPINION COUNTS!

Please check TRUE or FALSE below to express your opinion about the following statements:

Q1 Do you believe in "true love"?

"TRUE LOVE HAPPENS ONLY ONCE IN A LIFETIME."
○ TRUE
○ FALSE

Q2 Do you think marriage has any value in today's world?

"YOU CAN BE TOTALLY COMMITTED TO SOMEONE WITHOUT BEING MARRIED."
○ TRUE
○ FALSE

Q3 What kind of books do you enjoy?

"A GREAT NOVEL MUST HAVE A HAPPY ENDING."
○ TRUE
○ FALSE

YES, I have scratched the area below.

Please send me the 2 **FREE BOOKS** and **FREE GIFT** for which I qualify. I understand I am under no obligation to purchase any books, as explained on the back of this card.

© 2003 HARLEQUIN ENTERPRISES LTD. ® and TM are trademarks owned and used by the trademark owner and/or its licensees.

DETACH AND MAIL CARD TODAY!

335 SDL DZ32   235 SDL DZ4H

(S-SE-03/04)

FIRST NAME   LAST NAME

ADDRESS

APT.#   CITY

STATE/PROV.   ZIP/POSTAL CODE

www.eHarlequin.com

Offer limited to one per household and not valid to current Silhouette Special Edition® subscribers. All orders subject to approval. Credit or debit balances in a customer's account(s) may be offset by any other outstanding balance owed by or to the customer.

"No interference. Either I'll be called in or I won't. With luck we'll have the picnic."

"Well, okay. I was just surprised by your call."

"Yeah, me too."

He heard her chuckle. "At least you're still Honest Dan."

With that she said goodbye and hung up.

He found himself whistling as he put a frozen pizza in the microwave. Later, he put a picture of Fay and the baby up on the refrigerator door.

At work, on Saturday morning, he soon saw there would be no getting away today for any reason. As soon as he could take a break, he called Fay's number. Again Mrs. Monroe answered. "She had to go grocery shopping and the baby was asleep so I told her to go ahead and I'd stay over here 'til she came back. I can still remember what a hassle it was to shop with a baby in tow."

"Yes, well, would you please give her a message for me? I can't get away today."

"Oh, that's too bad. And it's going to rain tonight and tomorrow, so there's no hope for a picnic."

"Tell Fay I'll—" he began, but Mrs. Monroe cut him off.

"I've just had a wonderful idea. I do so hate to eat alone, especially when it's a Sunday dinner. That was always a family day. Why don't I roast a chicken for you and Fay to share with me and we can have a Sunday dinner picnic indoors?"

"That's kind of you, Mrs. Monroe, but—"

"You must call me Clara. I finally realized why you looked so familiar. You're the policeman who was wounded by that dreadful criminal. I saw your picture in the paper at the time. Please say you'll come to dinner. It's the least I can do for one of our brave officers.''

Once she put it like that, there was no graceful way to refuse. Dan accepted.

''Fine. I'll expect you at four.''

He hung up and shook his head. What had started out as a simple phone call to find out how Fay and Marie were getting along had escalated into a picnic and now into a Sunday dinner—with Clara Monroe present. Which probably was just as well.

When he arrived on the rainy Sunday, Fay opened the door to Clara's part of the house. His heart skipped a beat, but he covered up any emotion by handing her the flowers.

''Oh, these must be for Clara,'' she said. ''How thoughtful of you.''

They'd been for Fay, but he could hardly say so now.

Should have brought two bouquets. He did have the rattle for Marie, but he'd forgotten and left it in the car.

''You look great,'' he told Fay. An understatement.

''Thank you,'' she said.

How stiff they both sounded, he thought.

Clara came from the kitchen to greet him and accepted the flowers with delight.

''Dinner smells so good my mouth's watering,'' he told her. Because Clara was here, he and Fay wouldn't have to confront any unfinished business, which would make it easier for both of them.

He'd understood last night the reason he'd called Fay was because of that unfinished business. Until they resolved their relationship one way or the other, it wasn't over, but still pending like a case file that couldn't be closed because all the facts weren't in.

"Come see the baby," Fay said to him.

He followed her over to the alcove where Marie lay sleeping in the cradle. Looking down at the little girl he blurted out, "She's grown!"

"They do, you know."

"Yes, but so fast?" It'd only been two weeks, after all.

He'd been trying not to stare at Fay, who'd also changed in those two weeks. He'd never before seen her in a dress. Or with her hair the way it was. She was stunning. Sexy. Mouthwatering.

"Well?" she asked, making him realize he'd been staring despite himself.

"Have I now seen you at your best?" he managed to say, keeping it light.

"More or less."

"I'm overwhelmed." Which was close to the truth.

She smiled. "I doubt that."

He grinned at her. "How about impressed?"

"I certainly hope so."

Clara, who'd gone back to the kitchen, came in again, carrying a tray with three stemmed glasses and a wine bottle. "Sherry," she told them, setting it down on the coffee table. "Mother always served sherry before Sunday dinner. I got out of the habit when the children came along, but I decided this occasion called for it. Unless you'd prefer something else?"

Dan shook his head. When they all had a filled glass, he said, "To our Sunday picnic." They touched glasses, then sipped the wine. Dan didn't care much for sherry, but why should he disturb what was a fondly recalled ritual to Clara Monroe?

Fay wasn't much of a drinker, of sherry or anything else alcoholic. And she didn't want to risk drinking any now because she was nursing. But she pretended to sip the wine so Clara's feelings wouldn't be hurt.

She glanced at Dan, who, she saw, was trying to look as though he liked sherry. She'd done her best to convince herself it didn't matter that her pulse had speeded when she opened the door and saw him on the doorstep, but she'd failed. She had to face it, she was glad to see him.

He looked somehow different, perhaps because he was dressed less casually than at the cabin. He wore clothes well, she realized, dominating them instead of being dominated by them as some men were.

Had he liked the change in her? He certainly should have, since she'd had her hair styled, bought herself a new dress and taken extra pains with her makeup. For him, because he'd never seen her as she could be. Now he had. What did he think?

Danny Marie whimpered. Before Fay could rise from her chair, Dan sprang up and hurried to the cradle. The next moment he was back, the baby in his arms, gazing up at him as he murmured, "Hi, there. Miss me? I missed you. You've gone and grown on me while I wasn't looking."

The baby gurgled and smiled, almost as though she understood every word. Was it possible a child so young could recall a voice? Remember a face?

"Isn't that nice," Clara said. "So many men seem to be afraid to pick up babies." She rose. "I'll just take a look at the sweet potatoes."

"I can help," Fay offered.

Clara waved her back down. "No, not yet. I'll call you when I'm ready to set dinner on the table."

Dan brought the baby over to Fay, asking, "Is she hungry?"

Fay shook her head. "I fed her just before you came. She's getting quite sociable these days. When she hears voices, she wants to be part of what's going on."

Dan seated himself on the couch next to Fay, supporting the baby on his knees. "Smart kid. She acts as though she remembers me."

Since the baby was gazing up at Dan as though fascinated, Fay couldn't argue. "Don't forget, you're the first person she saw after she was born."

"I can never forget that." He spoke softly, without looking at her. "Or what we—"

Fay cut him off. "Let's talk about something else."

He shrugged. "Sooner or later."

She shook her head. "Never. What's past is past."

If she'd said the words casually or flatly, he might have decided she meant them, but the vehemence in her voice was a dead giveaway. She knew as well as he did they had unfinished business.

"What would you call it in your work?" he asked. "A closed file?"

"Perhaps."

"We keep unsolved case files open for years," he told her. "And that's what this is. Unsolved."

"I'm ready to put dinner on the table," Clara called from the kitchen.

Fay rose and hurried away so fast he wondered whether she might be trying to run from him.

"Your mama doesn't want to open her closed file," he told Marie as he gently jiggled her on his knees.

Having the baby close to him warmed his heart. He began humming to her, not at first conscious of the tune he'd picked until he finally realized it was "Bye Baby Bunting" again and stopped humming.

By the time Fay appeared again, to call him to the table, the baby was sleeping. Dan laid her in the cradle, covered her up and strode to the dining room.

He was relieved to see that Clara had already cut the chicken in the kitchen and that he wouldn't be faced with "carving" just because he was a man.

As they ate, he asked Clara how old the Monroe Mansion was and much of the conversation after that was about the old mansions still standing along these few blocks.

As they were finishing, the phone rang. Clara got up to answer it and, after a few minutes came back into the dining room looking flustered.

"That was my friend, Yvonne Tousignant," Clara said. "I'd completely forgotten that I'd promised to go to the movies with her this evening. I do hate to disappoint her, because I know she won't go alone."

"No problem," Dan said. "Go with her and enjoy the movie."

"But you and Fay will be left with all these dishes. Although I suppose you could just leave them for me to—"

"Don't worry about the dishes," Fay said. "I know for a fact Dan is an expert at cleaning up kitchens. The two of us will have everything done in no time. Do take in the movie, Clara."

"The least I can do is offer a helping hand after that wonderful meal you fixed," Dan said. "Your chocolate cake is the best I've ever eaten."

The older woman looked from one to the other of

them and finally gave them a conspiratorial smile. "I understand," she murmured. "After all, two's company..."

It wasn't long before her friend came by to pick her up and then Dan and Fay were left without Clara to chaperone them. Which suited him just fine, but seemed to rattle Fay because she immediately began busying herself with the dishes.

"What's the hurry?" he said.

"Well, they won't wash themselves." Fay sounded edgy.

"No, but the dishwasher will."

"I meant there's a lot of cleaning up to do."

"You didn't mean being alone with me makes you nervous?"

She shot him a defiant look. "That, too. We have no unfinished business to complete."

He raised an eyebrow. "You say that, but we do. How about if I agree to start with the unfinished business of the dishes and work up to the other?"

Instead of replying, she handed him a stack of dirty plates she'd stacked.

"Okay, I'll carry them to the kitchen and you load the dishwasher."

With two of them working side by side, the table was cleared, dishwasher turned on and the kitchen returned to its normal tidy state.

"I could make more coffee," Fay offered.

"Not for me."

"Maybe you'd like another slice of cake."

"Delicious as it was, no. What I *would* like is to know how you feel about us seeing each other."

She eased down onto one of the kitchen chairs. "It won't work."

He sat on another. "Why not?"

"Well, for one thing we're so different."

"I can't argue with that, since I'm a male and you're a female."

She frowned at him. "You know what I mean."

"No, I don't."

"Any relationship we might have could never last."

"So? Nothing lasts forever."

Glaring across the table at him, she snapped, "What is it you want, then—a one-night stand?"

"How can either of us ever find out what we want if you and I don't go on seeing each other?"

Fay rolled her eyes. "This discussion is ridiculous."

"So start a better one."

She took a deep breath and huffed it out. "Well, I suppose we can still be friends."

That made him chuckle.

She narrowed her eyes at him. "I'm serious."

"I guess we can give friendship a try, but you're evading the issue."

The baby started to whimper and Fay sprang up to go to her. Dan followed her into the living room, and watched Fay pick her up.

"She's hungry," Fay said, leaving the room with the baby and disappearing through a door.

Though Marie had grown, she was still tiny and helpless, needing her mother. Needing him? Dan wondered and sighed. Probably not, even though he felt he still wanted to be in her life.

Because Fay didn't return right away, he realized

she must be nursing the baby in another room. Just as well, since he wouldn't have been able to watch. Not anymore.

In Clara's guest bedroom, where she was nursing Danny Marie, Fay told herself it was just as well Clara had taken the picnic out of Dan's hands. She was far from sure they should ever see each other again, much less without another adult present. Actually, she really wasn't ready to date any man yet, even though her local doctor had said she could resume all her normal activities.

On Friday, a guy from the office where she was working had asked her to lunch. He was good-looking and seemed pleasant, but she didn't accept. She'd refused politely, while making it clear she wasn't interested.

She'd be lying if she said she wasn't interested in Dan. But interested didn't mean she'd date him. He was right about the unfinished business, that was no closed file. Not yet. Though she'd like to believe it one day would be.

When the baby was satisfied, she carried her back to the cradle and joined Dan in the living room.

"Monday morning comes early," she said, glancing at her watch.

"I'd be the last to deny that," Dan said. "I'm also good at taking hints."

She didn't know whether to be relieved or disappointed when he rose. Whatever she felt, she found herself walking with him to the entry.

"I know what you're going to say," he told her when they stood in front of the door.

"You do not."

"Don't call me, I'll call you."

This man had a way of making her smile when it was the last thing she intended to do. "Something like that, yes," she admitted.

"Okay." He leaned toward her and she held her breath, helpless to move away as she waited for his kiss. A kiss that never came.

Instead he straightened, touched her lips with his forefinger, then opened the door and stepped onto the porch. He looked back and added, "That was a reminder this is far from over." He shut the door before she had a chance to reply.

What would she have said, she asked herself as she made her way back to the baby. That he was wrong, that there was no place for them to go? That he was right and they had to find some solution? That she'd badly wanted the kiss he hadn't given her? That if he waited for her to call him, he'd wait forever?

Fay found she actually didn't know.

Chapter Nine

Not that she was counting, Fay told herself, but more than two weeks had gone by since Clara's dinner without a call from Dan. He must have meant what he said, that he wouldn't call again; it was up to her. Maybe he figured time would take care of all the loose ends, but she was no longer so sure.

Not that she intended to disturb the status quo. Commuting to her consulting job three days a week, trying to give her daughter quality time, plus errands and the work she had to do at home was enough for her to handle without complicating her life further.

As far as forgetting about Dan entirely, that wasn't possible, especially since Clara all too often mentioned "that nice young man."

Fay's father hadn't called either and that bothered her, though she knew it might be because he thought she was in Duluth. Apparently he hadn't tried Aunt

Marie's number or he would have known Marie was in California. Or maybe he had and decided Fay had gone there with Marie.

I don't care what my father thinks, she told herself. *He doesn't care about me, why should I care about him? He's got that woman he told me about to keep him company, the widow he wanted me to meet before he knew about my pregnancy.*

Though Fay knew she shouldn't begrudge her father finding a companion, neither had she cared to meet someone who would be more or less taking her mother's place.

A loud wail from Danny Marie reminded Fay the baby needed attention and that she'd better get with it or one of her precious days off from work would be gone before she'd accomplished anything.

An hour later, with the baby changed and fed, a load of clothes finishing up in the dryer and her list of shopping made out, Fay was in her bedroom dabbing on lip gloss when the door chime sounded. Could be the man Clara had said was coming by this week to give an estimate for replacing the tile around Fay's bathroom sink. She ran a brush through her hair and started for the door.

She glanced from the living room window as she passed by, seeing a car parked in front. Still thinking of the tile man, she opened the door and stared. Dan stood on the porch wearing faded jeans and a blue T-shirt with no logo. She struggled with a crazy urge to throw her arms around him.

"Going to ask me in?" he said after a moment.

"Um, sure." Heart pounding, she stepped aside and he entered.

After he closed the door he examined it, then

turned to her. "No chain. I'll put one on. Chains aren't foolproof, but they do let you look out and see who's there before you open the door. You should know who you're letting in."

"I thought you were the tile man," she blurted.

"Yeah, but I'm not. It's not safe these days, even in Archer, to take chances."

Gathering her wits, she said. "I wasn't expecting you."

"I figured unexpectedly was the best time to come. I have today off and you don't work on Tuesdays. Besides, I have a present for Peanut I forgot to give her." He gestured toward the window. "Sun's out. We can take her for a walk."

Did he think he could simply show up and find her ready to do anything he suggested? "I have clothes in the dryer and a long list of shopping to do and—"

"No problem. I'm a dab hand at folding clothes as you already know. As for the shopping—hey, I can do that, too. Where's the dryer?"

He grinned at her and she found herself unable to resist. "I admit I hate to fold clothes," she confessed.

With two of them working at it, the clothes were soon taken care of. "Now," he said, "for the shopping."

"We'll have to take my car because of the baby bed."

"No sweat. A friend gave me one—his kid outgrew it."

She gaped at him. "You actually have a baby bed in your car?"

"Yeah. Grab your list and I'll get Peanut."

Fay discovered shopping was fun with Dan along

to amuse the baby with the red rattle he'd bought her. Or maybe it was just because he was along, period. In what seemed like no time they were done, the last stop being a hardware store where he bought a chain for her front door. By the time he carried Danny Marie in, she was sound asleep.

After he placed her in the cradle, he reappeared and helped Fay lug in the groceries.

"It's noon," she said. "Will you stay for lunch? You've certainly earned it."

"Only if I can help. Hard to adjust to you waiting on me."

"I'm completely recovered," she said a trifle tartly.

He gave her an all-over glance that made her catch her breath. "I can see you are," he drawled.

Having Dan help her in the kitchen reminded her of their last few weeks in the cabin, when she'd been well enough to help him. Except now it felt more intimate than it had then. Her pulse pounded every time they almost touched as they worked together in the small kitchen.

When they sat down to their salad and sandwich lunch, he said, "I warned you that you hadn't seen the last of me."

"I know you promised not to call."

"Showing up isn't calling."

"A technicality."

He shook his head. "Remote versus within touching distance."

Bemused by his words and the look in his eyes, she paused with her fork halfway to her mouth. *Touching distance.* Forcing herself to snap out of it, she set down her fork and said, "I think you miss the baby."

"I miss—" He paused for a long moment. "I miss the cabin."

So did she. But that time was over for them both. "Forward is the only direction I go."

He shrugged. "Backtracking sometimes works on a case. The spooks have a saying—"

"Spooks?"

"Yeah, the FBI, CIA, those guys say, 'let's walk back the cat.' You can uncover facts you missed initially."

She grimaced. "We're not dealing with a case here. I don't think anything is missing."

"Maybe not. But are you sure?"

Fay picked up her water glass and deliberately took a long swallow to give her time to think. "Let's leave the cat alone," she said finally.

"I've got one," he said.

"One what?"

"Cat. Not that it was my choice. I opened the door last Monday, he walked in and won't leave."

She tried and failed to imagine Dan being dictated to by a cat. If anyone had asked her she would have told them he was more likely to have a dog.

"If you don't want the cat, why not just call the animal shelter? They—" His scowl stopped her.

"His name is Spot. In her animal rescue days, Megan always argued that you can't get rid of a stray you've already named."

"I always thought Spot was a dog's name."

"He's black with one white spot on his chest."

"So, okay, the name fits the cat. I think we've gotten off the subject somewhere here."

"Any dessert?"

His question made it obvious Dan had no intention

of returning to what they'd been talking about, so Fay pointed to the owl-shaped cookie jar on the counter. "Clara sent over some cookies she calls sandies. They're delicious."

Dan crossed to the cookie jar, opened it, grabbed a plate from the cupboard and dumped some sandies onto the plate. He set it on the table between them before reseating himself and taking a cookie. "Clara's one fine cook," he announced. "You're lucky to have her for a landlady."

"Where do you live?" Fay asked.

"Riverview Apartments."

"They let you keep pets there?"

"Evidently. No one's thrown me out yet. Don't you like cats?"

"I've never had a pet of any kind." Her mother had been adamant about that. No cats, dogs, birds, hamsters, not even a goldfish.

"Why not?"

"My mother said since she was the one who'd have to take care of them in the long run, she had the last word. She believed pets were more trouble than they were worth." Feeling a need to defend her mother, Fay added, "Didn't your mother ever complain about Megan's many strays?"

He shook his head. "She liked animals. Even the goat." He smiled. "But she did find homes for most of them pretty fast."

Dan's smile faded as quickly as it had come.

"How about that walk with Marie once we clean up the lunch dishes? I noticed a park near here. Or better still, we can drive over to the county park and walk along the paved trails."

"I've never taken her there," Fay said. "When I

was a Brownie we hiked those trails before they were paved. Then later—'' She broke off.

"Lover's Lane parking as a teen?" he asked.

She eyed him assessingly. "That's a wild guess. You didn't grow up in Archer."

"Don't forget I drove a squad car before I earned my detective badge, and we moved those couples on. Nowadays the gals parked anywhere at night have more to worry about than what the guy with them has in mind."

The baby demanded attention with a wail and Fay started to leave the kitchen.

"Wait," he said. "Let me change her while you finish up here."

"Anytime anyone offers to change a diaper, I'll take them up on it. There's a changing table and diapers in the nursery."

Dan lifted the fussing baby from the cradle, murmuring to her. He glanced around Fay's bedroom, noticing that he was nowhere as neat as she was. He breathed in the scent he associated with the time they'd been together in the cabin, some kind of distinctive cologne with a hint of roses, but also faintly spicy. Like Fay? He smiled, suspecting she could be a lot spicier than her cologne suggested, then had to fight off his body's immediate reaction to that thought.

"You know, Marie," he said as he carried her into the nursery, "your mama isn't like anyone else. You're too young to hear why, so I'll keep the details to myself."

She gurgled at him.

"Recognize me, do you?" he said, depositing her onto the changing table. "I guess you don't get to see many men. At least I hope not.'' It took him a minute to deal with the flash of jealousy that ripped through him at the thought of Fay with another man. He couldn't call her his, but he didn't want her to be anyone else's.

''Old Dan's got a problem he'll have to work on,'' he told the baby as he deftly removed the wet diaper, used a disposable wipe and slid a dry diaper beneath her. ''Never liked that dog in the manger story.''

Fay was just closing the dishwasher when they returned to the kitchen. ''She's all set,'' he said, handing the baby over. ''I noticed the crib in the nursery, but I guess you're still using the cradle.''

''She's growing so fast I know I'll have to shift her to the crib soon, but the cradle's so convenient there by my bed. I'll take her into the nursery to feed her and then we'll be ready to go.''

He finished cleaning up the kitchen while waiting, wondering if he'd ever get accustomed again to watching Fay nurse the baby without having lustful thoughts. He shook his head, unable to understand why that had changed so abruptly from Madonna and child to something entirely different.

Why was he here? To see the baby, yes, but mostly to be with Fay. What did he want from Fay? To be honest, not commitment of any kind, but to get her in bed. After that, what? What did a forward-moving woman have in common with a stationary man? Sex, maybe. For a time. How long? He moved his shoulders uneasily, sensing something wrong with the scenario, something he couldn't pin down.

He let the water out of the sink and wiped his hands on a paper towel. Why worry? Either Fay would or she wouldn't. If she did, they would go on from there for whatever time. If she didn't, then it was over before it began.

As they got into his car to drive to the park, Fay said, "You've got an easy-to-remember license plate. All those sixes."

"Haven't lost the car yet."

"It doesn't have a police logo on it."

"That's because it's mine. Older car, inconspicuous, new engine no one can see without lifting the hood. Doesn't attract attention. I like it that way."

The baby made an unintelligible comment from the back seat. "Glad you agree," he told her over his shoulder. "I value your opinion."

Fay giggled. "I forgot you always talk to her as though she understands every word."

When they'd parked and set the baby in the stroller, he insisted on pushing her.

Fay walked beside him, enjoying the sunshine and the wildflowers growing alongside the trail. The trees had grown taller than they used to be when she was a teen, but weren't nearly as big as those around the cabin had been. They were in a sort of woods, yes, but nothing like the wilderness in the Upper Peninsula.

"Do you ever miss not living where you grew up?" she asked.

"Sometimes."

"Could you find an equivalent job in Evergreen Bluff?"

He sighed. "If a Sorenson hadn't—" He paused and started over. "One of my brothers did something a long time ago that made eternal enemies of the entire Crosswell clan. Wouldn't matter, except Sherm

Crosswell is the acting sheriff of the county my hometown is in—Nonesuch—and so being a deputy under him is out of the question. I could apply for a state job, but troopers don't have any say in where they're stationed, so why do that?"

"There must be other counties up there besides Nonesuch."

"Yeah, but we're talking home town here. Nonesuch is the biggest county in the U.P., and the county seat, Ojibway, is smack on Lake Superior way up at the top of the county with Evergreen Bluff thirteen miles away. Close enough. The point is, Nonesuch takes up so much territory that the county seats in any of the other counties vary from fifty to a couple hundred miles away from my hometown. The U.P.'s several small cities have equally small city police forces. All of those pay a lot less than I make here and none of them are in Nonesuch County."

"So the salary is important to you."

He looked at her incredulously. "Why would you think otherwise?"

She could hardly tell him the truth, that she'd thought his lack of drive to go beyond his present rank meant he wasn't particularly interested in money. That was foolish of her, she realized. He enjoyed what he did, but at the same time he wanted to be paid a decent amount to do it.

"Um, I guess I figured if you wanted to live closer to home, you might be willing to work for less." At least that approached the truth in an oblique way.

"As a deputy under Crosswell, I would be making less, but I might consider being home worth it. I'm not sure."

"A two-family feud," she said. "I haven't run into

anything like that before. Individuals might hate you, but an entire family hating an entire other family? Awesome. Do the Sorensons return the hate?''

He shook his head. ''Much as I dislike admitting it, what happened was my brother's fault. But no lasting damage was done. Why the Crosswells still hold a grudge is beyond me. Sometimes small towns are like that.''

A squirrel chattered at them from an oak tree branch, clearly scolding them for invading his space. Fay smiled up at the squirrel. ''I don't suppose we'll see any animal in this park wilder than that. I still remember the day we came across the doe. And those awesome wolves.''

''Going backward in time?'' he teased. ''I thought that was taboo.''

''An occasional outstanding memory is permitted,'' she informed him.

''I'll tuck that away for future reference.''

She found herself enjoying this outing with Dan far more than the occasion warranted. Well, why not? They were friends, after all. Only friends? Fay straightened her shoulders. Yes, and only friends they would remain.

Still, was there any real harm in an affair, short-lived though it probably would be? It wasn't as though either of them believed themselves in love or were trying to trap the other into marriage. She glanced sideways at Dan, only to find him looking at her. He stopped and so did she, gazes locked. She found it hard to breathe.

''I—'' she began.

''I—'' he said in unison.

Both started to laugh, the moment passed, and they

walked on. What had he been going to say? she wondered. For that matter, what had she intended to say? Surely not something like "take me, I'm yours." Which was how she'd felt.

"You're smiling," he said.

"I suddenly realized I'd forgotten what I started to say to you."

He didn't reply, so she prodded him. "How about you? I promise not to interrupt this time."

He shrugged. "Wasn't important."

"Tell me anyway."

"Something about smelling the perfume in your room," he muttered. "The kind you use."

"My perfume?" She blinked at him, confused.

"Told you it wasn't important."

She knew it had been, but she couldn't find any reason. Unless the scent of her perfume could have reminded him of the time they'd waltzed in the cabin and he wanted more of the same. Like she did.

"I think it may be time to move the cradle into the living room," she said, translating her thought into words before she realized what she was doing.

He raised an eyebrow. "Any particular reason to mention it right now?"

"Um, I intend to start using the crib, so the cradle doesn't need to be in my bedroom any longer."

"Every time you say 'um' first, it means you're giving me a diluted version of what you mean."

"It does not!"

He grinned at her. "Then why are you blushing?"

"My color comes from a brisk walk in the fresh air," she said haughtily.

"So let's move the cradle into the living room as

soon as we get back to your place and see what happens,'' he said.

''Da—the baby might not like the crib.''

''Peanut is one cool customer.''

''She's only a baby. She might not understand she's outgrowing the cradle.''

He turned the stroller into a walk leading to a bench under a flowering cherry tree and stopped. ''This isn't about the baby.''

She looked into his eyes and was caught in their blueness. ''No,'' she admitted. ''But I'm not sure—''

''Who is?'' As he spoke, a pink petal drifted down from the tree and caught in his hair. Without thinking, Fay reached up to remove it and found herself in his arms.

His mouth covered hers and she gave herself up to the remembered pleasure of the kiss. Neither Ken nor any other man had ever made her feel such a hammer of desire from a single kiss. So why wasn't she sure? She wanted Dan, no doubt about it. Why not go with the flow even if it wasn't meant to be forever?

His hands moved down to cup her bottom, pressing her close, letting her feel his need for her. She clung to him, relishing the moment with its tantalizing promise of fulfillment. But not here. Not now.

He lifted his head, loosening his hold. ''Still not sure?'' The rasp of passion in his voice thrilled her.

''Maybe we should see what happens,'' she murmured.

He released her, then plucked several pink petals from her hair. ''Showering us with blessings?'' he asked.

''You must be a secret romantic,'' she said, trying to come down from her high.

"Never been accused of that before." He turn to the stroller. "What do you think, Marie?"

The baby looked up at him wide-eyed. "Still got your blue eyes, I see," he said to her.

"My doctor says they show no sign of changing, so they'll probably stay that color." It seemed appropriate to Fay that Danny Marie's eyes should be blue, like her namesake's.

"Anyone in your family with blue eyes?"

"My father," she admitted reluctantly. Disturbed at the thought, she glanced at her watch. "We ought to be getting back. I have work to do."

"On your day off?"

"Always. I'm used to working a five-day week, so I have to keep up."

"You can't adjust the work to fit your three-day schedule?"

Fay shook her head and he shot her a skeptical look.

"It's just not how I operate," she added.

"High-powered."

Taking the flatness of his tone as a criticism, she snapped, "I didn't get where I am by slacking off."

They drove back to her apartment in silence.

"Still want me to move the cradle?" he asked as he pulled up in front.

"I suppose so." She heard the sullen tone in her voice with dismay. But she couldn't help it. Dan just didn't understand.

Inside, he deposited the baby in the crib and stood looking down at her. On the crib's opposite side, Fay stared at her daughter.

"She looks smaller than she did in the cradle," he said.

Fay nodded. "Maybe it's too soon."

He shifted his gaze to look at her. "You think so."
It wasn't a question.

"We're talking about my daughter here," she said,
"Are we?"

She knew they were and they weren't. While she
was still searching for words, he spoke, not to her,
but to the baby.

"Time for me to say goodbye. Keep growing, little
one." He reached down and gently ruffled the baby's
blond hair.

"Thanks for the lunch," he told Fay. "Don't know
when I'll have time to stop by again." At the door
of the nursery he turned and added, "But this isn't
the last you'll see of me."

Fay didn't follow him out until she heard the front
door close. Hurrying to the window, she saw his car
pulling away from the curb. Damn the man.

Every time they were together he stirred emotions
in her she wasn't ready to feel. Physically maybe, but
not mentally. It was like she feared she might come
to feel something more than she wanted to for that
Viking who'd just left.

Chapter Ten

The following Monday, soon after Fay got home from work, her client called her.

"Sorry to bother you, but something has come up that I need to discuss with you. I'd like to have input on this before I leave for New York on Wednesday. Could you come in for a few hours tomorrow? Say about ten?"

Ordinarily she would have said yes without thinking, even though Tuesday was one of her days off, but this past week she'd been mulling over how she wanted to handle future contracts. "Could we possibly discuss this on the phone?" she asked.

"Not really. I need you to look over some papers first."

"Then I'll give you a tentative yes," she told him. "If anything comes up to change things, I'll let you know."

She sighed as she hung up, thinking she may as well face the fact that her attitude toward work was changing. Being a mother made more of a difference than she'd have believed before Danny Marie was born. She actually resented having to go to work on her day off, whereas before it rarely had fazed her. To get ahead, she had to come up with extras. Not that she'd changed her mind about getting ahead.

High-powered.

Dan's comment echoed in her mind. Well, if that's what it took, she was. It wasn't her fault if he didn't see it as a positive.

The phone rang again and she frowned at it before answering. What now?

"You may have noticed I hurried away the minute you came in," Clara said. "I need to explain why."

Actually Fay hadn't paid that much attention, but she didn't say so.

"I want you to know I found an old mask left over from the last time I painted my bathroom and I wore that every time I came near the baby," Clara said.

"Mask?" Fay asked. "What for?"

"Right after you left for work, I started sneezing and worried I was coming down with a cold. I didn't want to take any chances. I washed my hands every time before I touched her, too."

"Every sneeze isn't a cold."

"I realize that, dear, but now my throat's a little raw and my nose has begun to run. I ate lunch with my cousin on the weekend and she had a terrible cold. I didn't think much about it at the time, but I must have caught it from her. I do hope Danny Marie won't be affected." Clara coughed and apologized.

"It does sound like you've caught cold," Fay agreed.

"I hate to disrupt your schedule, but I don't think I'd better come near the baby until I'm over this. If you like, I'll call up a friend of mine who often sits for her grandchildren and ask her if she can take my place on Wednesday and Friday. She's a most reliable person. You've met her...Yvonne Tousignant."

"That's very kind of you. I do remember her. But, actually, I'd need her to come in tomorrow for a few hours as well."

"I'll call Yvonne this minute and let you know if she can help," Clara said.

Why was it that problems always arrived one on top of another? Fay wondered while she changed into jeans and a T-shirt. If Yvonne wasn't willing to pinch-hit for Clara, Fay would be, as her father used to say, rooky-dooed. There was no way she'd let a total stranger take care of her daughter.

Clara called back shortly. "Yvonne will be happy to substitute for me on Wednesday and Friday, but she can't help you out tomorrow because she has a dental appointment she doesn't want to cancel."

"Thanks so much, Clara—you're a life-saver."

"But what will you do about tomorrow?"

"Don't worry about that. Just rest and get over your cold. I'll figure out something."

After mulling it over while she changed and fed Danny Marie, Fay decided that, since she was going in tomorrow at the request of the client, he'd just have to put up with her bringing the baby. She didn't much care for the idea, but it was the only solution she could come up with.

In the morning, the phone rang while Fay was gathering baby supplies to take with her. She snatched it up, wondering what new calamity would descend.

"We need to talk," Dan said. I—"

"I can't talk now," Fay said. "I'm on my way to work and Clara's sick so I have to take the baby."

She expected him to say something about it being Tuesday and her day off.

Instead, he said, "I'll be right over."

"I can't wait, I have to get going."

"You going to make me use the siren?"

She hadn't realized he had a siren in his car. Envisioning him pulling up to the curb, siren screeching, which would disturb Clara, Fay sighed. "I'll wait five minutes."

Dan parked in front of the house with seconds to spare. He leaped out and strode to her door. Fay opened it before he got there, dressed in a dark blue business suit. "You look very efficient," he said, edging past her into the entry.

She eyed him balefully. "I don't know why you bothered to come over when I told you I had to leave."

"Don't you recognize a capable baby-sitter when you see one?"

"But, aren't you working?"

"Day off. Just tell me how to feed Marie and you're outta here."

"I—you—"

"Breast milk bottled in the refrigerator?" he said. "Or are you using formula when you don't nurse her?"

"Breast milk. I suppose it's all right." She sounded doubtful.

"Think about who took care of her in the cabin."

She nodded. "She'll be better off here with you than stuck in an office with me, that's for sure. I should be back around one. Thanks, Dan. I owe you."

"I'll keep that in mind," he said as he watched her pick up her briefcase.

She started for the door, turning back to say, "If you need to reach me, the number where I'll be is on the front of the refrigerator."

"Don't worry. We'll be fine."

After she left, Dan wandered into the living room and smiled when he saw the cradle in a corner, filled with stuffed animals. In the nursery, the baby lay in the crib waving her hands and making noises at a colorful mobile above her. When he came up to the crib, she focused on his face and smiled.

Did she recognize him? he wondered, hoping she had. He had no idea how old babies had to be before they knew a familiar face from a strange one.

Lifting her from the crib, he cradled her in one arm. "It's your old friend, Dan," he told her, "come to take care of you again. You might not understand me, but you sure do listen." He could hear the fondness threading through his words and decided she could, too, and that was all she needed to understand right now.

Carrying the baby, he ambled through the apartment, studying the titles of Fay's books, her CDs and examining the paintings hung on the walls and the photos in frames on one of the built-in shelves between the windows. One caught his attention—a little girl standing between two adults. Fay, as a child, probably with her parents. Her father, a stocky blond man was smiling down at his daughter, while her brown-haired mother gazed straight at the camera, her expression seeming to dare the picture-taker to press the button.

He looked at the photo for a long time. From what Fay had told him about her father, he'd have expected him rather than her mother to be staring unsmiling at the camera. Still, his experience with his own parents had taught him you couldn't ever be sure what went on in their heads. He didn't think he'd ever seen a photo of his mother where she hadn't been smiling. When he'd been home last Christmas, though, Megan had pointed out their mother's smile in the pictures was often wistful. He sighed and turned away.

There'd been no photo of any man the right age to have been Ken. Dan was surprised to feel a flash of regret that the man would never know he had a daughter, never hold her, never watch her grow. He shook his head.

On the other hand, Dan Sorenson cared about this little girl. The weight of her warm little body against his arm and chest felt not only familiar, but right. In a way she was his. Hadn't he helped her to be born? Wasn't he the first person to hold her? Hadn't she given him her first smile? Hell, he'd even changed her first wet diaper.

Later, when he sat in the nursery rocking chair feeding the baby a bottle and humming softly, a strange feeling crept over him. Yes, Marie was his in a way, but so was her mother. He had no right to either of them, and yet…

Damn, he was humming the "Bye Baby Bunting" song again. Didn't he know any other lullabies?

He burped Marie, then laid her on his knees to look at her. "Are you sleepy?" he asked. "Old Dan needs some time to put that chain on your mama's door."

She waved her hands and kicked with her feet. "Okay, I guess that means you're not." He lifted her up against his shoulder and rose, intending to put on one of Fay's CDs. He'd gotten as far as the living room when the doorbell rang.

Once a cop, always a cop. Swinging around, he called out gruffly, "Who's there?"

"Hank Merriweather," a man's voice answered. "Who the hell are you? And where's Fay?"

Fay's father? The man who disowned his granddaughter before she was born? The last Dan had heard he and Fay hadn't reconciled, but that'd been a week ago. Without answering, he walked to the door and opened it. The stocky man from the photo, older and balding, stared back at him. Dan stood aside, offering room for Merriweather to enter.

When the older man was inside, Dan shut the door. Merriweather continued to stare at him, obviously taken aback. On impulse, Dan held out Marie. "Your granddaughter," he said. "Fay's working."

Merriweather hesitated, then took the baby, who promptly spit up on him. To Dan's surprise, Merriweather smiled. Ignoring the blob of milk, he said, "Fay used to do the same thing when she was a baby. Always spitting up on me, she was." He held the baby away from him to look at her. "Must be this one takes after my daughter instead of that hockey puck. I know he's dead, but that doesn't make him less of a jerk." Cuddling the baby to him, he frowned at Dan, "Who are you?"

Dan was tempted to say, "The baby-sitter," but, before he could speak Merriweather cut him off.

"Wait—I've seen you somewhere before. A picture in a newspaper. It'll come to me. Drugs. Cops.

That's it! You're the hero who killed that bastard after he shot you. Your name's Dan something. Sorenson. Dan Sorenson. How's your leg?''

"Pretty much back to normal," Dan said, his negative view of the man altering slightly.

Shifting the baby, Merriweather held out his hand. "Glad to meet you, Dan."

Not to shake Fay's father's hand would be an insult, so Dan obliged.

"So now I know who you are," Hank said, "but that doesn't explain what the hell you're doing in my daughter's apartment."

"It's a long story, Mr. Merriweather," Dan said. "But to shorten it, I'm here today as a baby-sitter."

"Might as well call me Hank." He held the baby away from him again. "Pretty little thing, isn't she? So was Fay. Always had a mind of her own, though. So she's working." He shook his head. "Needs to play some is what I always told her. More to life than work. Any coffee in this place?"

Since he could hardly throw the man out, Dan led the way to the kitchen where Hank promptly sat at the table. By the time Dan got the coffee started, Marie was beginning to fuss.

"Maybe you better take her," Hank said.

Dan lifted the baby from her grandfather's lap and carried her into the nursery where he changed her, then settled her into the crib, jiggling it a little until her eyes drooped shut.

When he got back to the kitchen Hank had found and filled two coffee mugs. "So you're baby-sitting," he said. "Seems an odd chore for a cop. I got time, so you better fill me in on the long version of why."

Dan decided to give it to him hard and straight.

"Fay left Archer, heading for her aunt in Duluth. She knew you didn't want her to have the baby, so she wanted to be somewhere she'd feel welcome."

Hank grunted. "Figured that's where she's been. Doesn't explain where you came from, though."

"Fay didn't make it to Duluth, she got caught in a spring storm in the U.P. Meanwhile her Aunt Marie had flown to California because her daughter was in an accident."

"Some hodgepodge."

"You could say that and more. Fay ran her car into a tree in the blizzard a ways from the cabin where I'd gone to recuperate."

"What's that you're saying...cabin? Whereabouts?"

"Nonesuch County."

"I've been hunting up there. Nothing but wilderness. You mean to tell me my little girl had to wander around in a storm in that forsaken place?"

"By the time she found my cabin she was in labor."

Hank stared at him. "Good God!"

"Pretty much what I said at the time. We were snowed in by then, no chance to get out. Then the electricity and phone line went out."

"You mean to say you..." Hank's words trailed off.

Dan shrugged. "Neither she nor I had any choice. Luckily everything turned out okay, except that Fay developed anemia."

"My poor little girl." Hank blinked rapidly. "I didn't mean to put her through all that. Didn't mean to drive her away. Just couldn't take to that fellow of hers and I figured it'd be too much of a burden on her to raise his kid. Always wanted the best for my daughter. How's she doing now?"

"My brother's a doctor up there and I took her to him when the storm ended. He gave her what was needed and she's fine."

"I guess she must be if she's back at work. But I still don't see why you're here. I admit you seem to be a long sight better than dipstick ever was, but…" He paused, frowning at Dan.

"I'm here because the baby's regular sitter has a cold and it happened to be my day off."

"You don't live here then?"

Dan had enough of the inquisition. "If I did, it wouldn't be any of your business."

Hank's glare faded and he sighed. "Bullheaded, that's me. I guess I turned her against me for good. Didn't want that. One look at that little granddaughter of mine and I see I was about as wrong as a man can be."

"You hurt Fay."

Hank nodded and sighed again. Then he half smiled. "If I know my daughter, I made her mad as hops. Got a mind of her own, always did have. Think she'll ever forgive me?"

Dan shrugged. "That's up to her." As for him, he was thawing rapidly. Hank had been wrong, now he was admitting it. His regret was clear in his actions and words. It was easy to see he really did care about Fay. Cared a lot, enough to worry that she'd gotten tangled up with another wrong man. The problem was, Hank might be right about him.

"I left a message on Fay's answering machine a month ago," Hank went on, "asking her to please call me. She never did, and I figured maybe she wouldn't talk to me on the phone, so I came over here today to apologize for what I said and find out how she was doing.

"You know, a father can't help trying to interfere to protect his daughter. Never liked that guy she got herself engaged to. Thought she'd come to her senses when she told me she wasn't going to marry him, after all. Then he up and died. Figured it was all over. Wasn't. I couldn't stand to see her having to carry that jerk's baby, then have to raise it all by herself... We had a big fight, she being as bullheaded as me."

"She does have strong opinions," Dan admitted. "But I figure you were out of line."

"Yeah, like I said, I was wrong. I know I hurt her. Any idea when she's coming home?"

"Around one, she told me."

Hank looked at his watch. "Getting on for noon. Guess I'll stay here and wait. You like pizza?" Without waiting for an answer, he reached into his pocket for a cell phone, smiling when he looked at it. "Fay gave me this Christmas before last. Told me everyone had one and she wanted to make sure I wasn't going to be the last holdout. She always thinks I'm behind the times." He began to punch in numbers, saying, "I know a great pizza place that delivers."

When he finished the order, he put away the phone and looked across the table at Dan. "Never figured I'd find a hero cop baby-sitting my daughter's baby. But, hey, the kid's safe with you, anyway."

"Always." He wanted to add that Fay was, too, but how did he know that was the truth?

Hank shook his head, muttering, "I can't get over the danger she put herself in. Stubborn, that's what she is. Always was. Could have killed herself and that baby, too. Just goes ahead and jumps into things without asking for advice.'' He sighed. ''Guess I'm to blame for her taking off like that, though. After what I said, I'd be the last person she'd turn to.''

Since Hank *was* partly to blame and since, to Dan's own personal knowledge, Fay did tend to take risks, Dan couldn't disagree.

''She was never a gal to hold a grudge forever, though,'' Hank said. ''So I got a chance.'' He gave Dan a long look. ''Seems like you and Fay got to be pretty good friends.''

Dan heard a father's eternal question in Hank's words, the ''what-are-your-intentions-toward-my-daughter'' one.

''*Just* friends, yes.'' The truth. He might want more, but that hadn't happened yet and maybe never would.

''Hmm. Too bad. She could do worse.''

Dan hid his surprise. Her father had decided he was okay? Better not tell him that marriage wasn't for Dan Sorenson. That was definitely not the right response at the moment. ''She's pretty caught up in her work,'' he said finally.

''Her mother was always after her to get ahead and Fay listened to her. Luella was a wonderful woman and I guess I disappointed her by not wanting to get ahead any more than I was.'' Hank spread his hands. ''A man's what he is. Luella could never understand that.''

Dan did. Unwilling to face any more revelations, he switched the topic to sports and Hank seemed more than willing to go there with him.

The pizza arrived, Hank insisted on paying for it,

and together they finished it off. The box, empty of all but crumbs, was sitting in the middle of the kitchen table when Fay arrived home.

She stood in the archway to the kitchen staring from one man to the other in total disbelief. Her father and Dan sharing a pizza? Talking amicably?

Hank rose. "I came by to apologize," he said. "You were right and I was wrong. If I call you, will you let me come again?"

"I—I guess so," she stammered, unused to hearing her father ever apologize for anything.

"We'll talk things over then." He reached out as if to hug her, but then drew back. "You're looking real good, honey," he said. "Bye for now."

Fay watched him let himself out, still feeling stunned. "How did all this come about?" she asked Dan, gesturing toward the empty pizza box.

"You mean why did your father admit he was wrong? Grandpa Hank fell in love with his grand-daughter when she spit up on him."

"Because she spit up on him? That doesn't make sense."

"Apparently as a baby you used to spit up on him all the time."

It did make a crazy kind of sense, but she knew Dan must be leaving out quite a bit of what had gone on.

"Sorry we didn't save you any pizza."

"That's okay, the boss had sandwiches and soft drinks sent in. What did my dad have to say to you?"

"He wanted to know why I was here and how come we were friends. I told him some of it."

"Some of it?"

"You think I'm going to tell a father that I'm trying to seduce his daughter?"

Fay smiled. "Is that why you called me this morning?"

"I intended to ask you very politely if I could darken your door long enough to put on the chain."

"Is that all?"

"A guy always hopes for more."

"Instead you wound up baby-sitting and having to entertain my father." She chuckled. "Poor Dan."

"The chain still needs to be put on. I'll take care of that now."

Fay was still smiling when she entered her bedroom to change into something more casual. Though jeans and a T-shirt were her usual choice, she opted for an olive-green cotton skirt with a pale green shirt. Before redressing, since she'd gone over four hours without nursing, she unfastened her bra and used the breast pump, filling a bottle half full of milk to relieve her breast fullness. Once dressed again, she peeked in the nursery to check on Danny Marie and found her sleeping, then placed the bottle in the refrigerator. Back in the living room, she saw her front door now boasted a chain. Dan was just putting his tools away.

"Did you have some reason for believing you could seduce me?" she asked.

He left the tools in a canvas holder on the floor and rose to face her, nodding toward the cradle containing the stuffed animals. "Saw that."

"I moved it when I discovered the baby seemed to like the crib."

He took a step toward her. "Should I believe that?"

"I certainly wouldn't have taken her out of the cradle if she hadn't adjusted so quickly to the crib."

He took another step toward her. "And that was your only reason for shifting the cradle's location from your bedroom to the living room?"

"Um…" she began, broke off and covered her mouth with one hand.

He grinned at her and took two more steps, now near enough to touch her if he put out a hand. "Give it up. We both know what the move means."

"Yes, but—"

"What?"

"You sort of stormed out of here last Tuesday."

"Still mad about that? Your father tells me you don't hold grudges."

True. She had no trouble at all flaring up about something, but found it hard to hang on to anger very long. Still, she wasn't sure she was ready to forgive her father. The hurt had gone too deep.

"Tell you what," Dan said. "We'll put on a CD and dance."

The idea appealed to her.

"I think I saw a waltz among your CDs," he added. "Something about Vienna." He took her hand and led her toward the player.

"Vienna Nights," she murmured as he shuffled through the CDs, picked one out, slid it in and turned on the machine. The music began.

"I don't have a uniform on so this will have to do." He bowed. "May I have the honor?"

"My skirt is rather short for a ball gown, but I'll follow suit." She curtsied. "It will be my pleasure, sir."

Putting an arm around her, he whirled her into the

dance. "Did I happen to mention that the color of your gown changes your eyes to the deep green of summer leaves?"

She swallowed, touched by his words. Unlike other men she'd known, Dan didn't spout idle compliments. But, determined to keep things light, she said, "I feared you might compare them to a pond where algae grew."

Dan chuckled, drawing her closer. "Your eyes are nowhere near pond-scum green."

She laughed and leaned against him as he spun her around the room, the addictive familiarity of his scent taking her back to the cabin, to the tinny sound of a wind-up phonograph, to the waltz where he'd first kissed her.

"Dan," she murmured, "do you remember?"

"Everything," he whispered into her ear.

The warmth of his breath was transformed into a sizzle along her nerves. She raised her head to look into his face. "Ocean blue," she murmured.

He raised an eyebrow.

"Your eyes. The color of the ocean where it's deep."

"Thanks for not suggesting they remind you of, well, cyanosis."

A giggle escaped her lips. "You cops pick up strange words. I bet that's what you thought about me when you saw me standing on your cabin porch in the storm."

He shook his head. "You were only on the verge of turning blue." He whirled her around the room again before adding, "There's a lot to be said for 78 rpm records."

"There is?"

''They're short. I get the feeling this CD is never going to end. So, there's no choice but trying to waltz while—'' He broke off and lowered his mouth to hers.

Warm and insistent, his lips coaxed her to respond. Since she'd been anticipating the kiss for what seemed like ages, she did. The kiss quickly escalated until they were forced to abandon any pretense of dancing.

The press of his arousal against her body turned her insides to liquid. Any doubts she might have had about allowing their relationship to intensify burned to ashes in the heat of her desire.

Making love with Dan was what she wanted. Why else had she shifted the baby to the crib and moved the cradle from her bedroom? To be honest, she'd wanted him ever since that first kiss in the cabin.

Chapter Eleven

With the waltz music drifting after them, Dan lifted Fay into his arms and carried her into her bedroom. He eased her down until she sat on the edge of the bed, bent and removed the sandals she wore. Then he sat beside her and took off his own shoes and socks before tumbling them both onto the bed.

How habits learned in childhood stuck, he thought bemusedly as he pulled her into his arms. Even in the fierce grip of desire. He couldn't recall ever wanting a woman as intensely as he wanted Fay, yet he'd paused to obey the Sorenson house rule of never climbing into bed with shoes on. He'd even taken hers off—which was a lot more erotic than removing his own.

His lips claimed hers and her eager response blocked out the surroundings until there was only the two of them. As his tongue invaded her mouth he realized his need to claim her so thoroughly she wouldn't be able to tell where she ended and he began. A corner of his mind sent up a red flag, but he ignored the warning. Nothing mattered but to hold and caress her, to ignite her passion to match his.

Clothes—both his and hers—were in the way. With her help, he removed everything until they lay naked together. He controlled his body's urgent demand for immediate satisfaction. He'd waited for this a long time and so had she. And he'd damn well do everything in his power to make it as perfect as he could.

He ran his hand over the curve of her hip to cup her bottom, pressing her against his arousal, her pleasure moan heating his blood.

"Dan," she whispered. "Oh, Dan…"

Reaching between her thighs with his fingers, he found her ready, but he delayed entering her and continued stroking her until she was gasping. He started to reach into his pant pocket for protection, but Fay stopped him, murmuring she was on the Pill.

When he finally rose over her, she wrapped her legs around him, pulling him into her welcoming warmth. As they began the age-old waltz of passion, he was overcome by a wave of pleasure combined with need so intense that everything else blurred. Just when he could no longer hold back, he felt her contract around him, heard her cry out. Dan then thrust harder and faster until he joined her in a shattering release.

Afterward, they lay on their sides, still in each other's arms, savoring the afterglow. Finally, he rose up on one elbow, looked down at her and said, "You know, that wasn't the first time I undressed you."

"In the cabin," she said. "I only vaguely remember. I must have been a sight to see, nearly cyanotic."

He stroked his hand over her belly. "I have to say your shape was a lot different."

"What did you think, seeing me then?"

"Lust was not on my mind. Worry was, verging on panic when you told me the baby was coming."

"You seemed so calm."

"I didn't want to scare you."

"You didn't. I knew you'd help me."

He lifted his hand to her face, holding his palm against her cheek, then leaned down and kissed her, gently at first, then with increasing enthusiasm.

A sound, one he didn't at first recognize, penetrated his haze of rising desire. Not music. That must have ended long ago. Then he knew. The baby.

He drew back, but when she started to sit up, he said, "No, stay here, let me bring her to you."

Padding barefoot into the nursery, he picked up the now wailing baby, changed her diaper and carried her into the bedroom. Fay had thrown back the coverlet and had the sheet drawn up to her waist, propping herself up on pillows.

She took a long look at him at he approached the bed and smiled. "Unlike you with me, I never had the chance to see you naked before. I really never expected to be looking at a naked man carrying a baby."

"Like what you see?"

"My lips are sealed."

"Wait 'til Marie's fed. I've got a sure-fire method for unsealing lips." He handed her the baby, climbed under the sheet and lay back on a pillow.

"You're not going to run off and hide while I nurse?" she asked as she arranged the baby at her breast. "You didn't in the beginning, but then you changed."

"Something changed between us."

"And now?"

He didn't know what his reaction would be, but he figured now he could manage to handle whatever emotion emerged.

"Now is different." After a moment he added, "I was afraid to touch your breasts when we made love. I didn't know if I might—well, damage the milk supply or something."

She chuckled. "You might have gotten milk on your fingers, but you wouldn't have hurt me."

Her breasts were full and beautiful, the nipple he could see, large and erect. On impulse, he ran his forefinger over the nipple and drew it back wet with milk. Lifting the finger to his mouth, he licked it off. The taste was unremarkable, but it wasn't the taste that rocked him, it was the emotion thrilling through him. What was it? Not lust. Not desire. Not a longing to be like the baby, sucking milk from a mother's breast. It was as though he'd shared an intimate part of Fay.

A red flag waved wildly. What was he getting into here? He'd wanted to make love to her, sure, and what had happened between them was more than he'd ever expected. But sex was sex. He didn't need other emotions, whatever they might be, cluttering up his mind.

Get out of here, Sorenson, he told himself.

"What's the matter?" Fay asked.

"Nothing."

"You had the strangest look on your face for a minute there."

Tell her you have to leave, he urged himself. *Invent a meeting or something.* Instead, he closed his eyes, shutting off the picture of Fay, flushed and lovely, nursing the baby.

"Did my dad talk about this woman he's involved with?" Fay asked after a time.

"No."

"I know he wants me to meet her. She's a widow with a grown daughter. But I'm not sure I care to."

Surprised, Dan opened his eyes. "Why not?"

"I realize Mom's been dead for years, but I—well, seeing another woman with Dad seems wrong, somehow."

"Dog in the manger," he muttered.

She frowned. "No, not that. Dad has every right to choose a companion. But I'm not even sure yet that I can forgive him enough for a reconciliation. Even if I was sure, to do that, I'd have to meet this Nell Yates."

"Right."

She sighed and he closed his eyes again as though to shut out the fact he was still naked in bed with Fay instead of on his way out of here. If he had any sense, he'd be halfway home by now. But he couldn't make himself move. He must have dozed off briefly, because when he opened his eyes again, Marie was lying on the bed between them with Fay, the sheet pulled up above her breasts, jiggling the red rattle over her. The baby made excited passes at the rattle, none of which connected.

"I got red," he said, "because a TV show I caught while channel surfing claimed babies see primary colors best."

"She does like it." Glancing at him, Fay added, "Doesn't this seem sort of weird to you?"

"The rattle?"

"No. Did you ever imagine the three of us would be in bed together?"

"Two of us, maybe. Peanut's an extra."

Fond as he was of the baby, that's what she was at the moment. Extra. He leaped out of bed, picked up Marie and returned her to the crib. He got back into bed and reached for Fay.

Fay snuggled into his arms, where she was beginning to feel she belonged. Making love with Dan had exceeded her most heated imaginings and one time was definitely not enough.

He pulled down the sheet so there was nothing between them. His mouth next to her ear, he whispered, "I told you once you were beautiful and you didn't believe me."

"That was in the cabin. I wasn't."

"You were and you are. I like to look at you." His hand slid over to caress her breast and then ease down over her hip. "Even better, I like to touch you."

"Mmmm," she murmured, rubbing against him. She slipped her hand between them and ran it along his belly, feeling his muscles contract under her fingers. She let her hand drift down until she felt his arousal. "Thought so," she said.

"What else, considering I'm in bed with my favorite naked woman?"

Favorite for the moment anyway, she tried to tell herself as his words and his touch tingled along her spine. "And here I thought this Tuesday was going to be a total loss," she said. "I—"

His kiss stopped her words, her thoughts and her

breath. How could a kiss be so powerful as to render her helpless, a victim of her own desire? She wanted to feel him inside her again. And again and again. Maybe that's why she'd kept backing away from making love with Dan. Because she'd feared the strength of her own feelings. For someone who prided herself on always being in control of any situation, this was scary. But too wonderful to miss.

Didn't every woman deserve one wild love affair in her life, however hopeless its permanence might be? Who needed permanence anyway?

Giving in to the pleasure of his caresses, Fay caressed him in turn, reveling in the feel of his skin under her fingers, thrilling to the wordless sounds that told her how much he enjoyed her touch.

She was more than ready when they finally came together and took each other up and up until they reached the peak. They held each other on the way down and afterward. She was drifting off to sleep when his beeper went off.

Dan jumped from the bed, scrambling among his discarded clothes on the floor until he reached the beeper and shut it off. She heard him swearing. ''Got to call the office,'' he muttered.

She sat up, realizing the day had drifted into evening. ''Whatever it is, I'll have to go,'' Dan said. ''They don't call me when I'm off duty unless it's important.'' He leaned to her, gave her a quick kiss, swept up his clothes and left the bedroom.

She stayed where she was until he called, ''Put the chain on,'' and she heard the front door close behind him.

She rose, tied her robe on and padded out to maneuver the chain into its slot. Then she head Danny

Marie fussing. Fay lifted her daughter from the crib to change her. Since the baby didn't seem hungry yet, Fay sat in the rocking chair, cuddling the baby and murmuring to her.

"Your mama has been very foolish," she told her daughter. "But do you know—I don't care. Getting ahead's important, but so is—" She stopped abruptly, aware the word that hovered on the tip of her tongue—love—was one she couldn't possibly mean. Didn't mean. Love had nothing to do with what had happened with Dan, wonderful though that had been.

"I know I love you, little one," she said. "And I suppose deep down I love my dad, mad as he makes me sometimes. Aunt Marie, too, and my cousin and her sons. But no one else."

There was no other family to love. Both her mother and father had been orphaned by the time they met. Though her mother had the one sister, Dad had been an only child. Like she'd been. "Like you'll be," she told the baby. Marriage and more children were just not on the agenda.

When Fay got home from work the next day, Yvonne had a message for her. "Your father called and asked that you give him a ring back when you can."

"Thanks. Any other messages?"

Yvonne shook her head. "I checked with Clara to see how she is and she does have a really bad cold. She asked if I could help you out on Monday if she didn't improve by then and it happens I can."

Fay thanked Yvonne for her willingness to help. After the woman had left, she found herself thinking about her father's message and that there had been no other calls. But Dan had been working today, too, and probably hadn't had a chance.

She hesitated before phoning her father, but after all, she had agreed he could call her. She sighed and punched in his number.

He spent several minutes telling her how sorry he was for being so bullheaded, and that he'd been wrong to try to convince her not to carry the baby. "I keep trying not to interfere in your life, but I keep doing it," he admitted. "I'm going to change that."

Then he went on about how the baby had reminded him of Fay as an infant. "You did right and I was wrong," he said.

She felt her anger seep away as she listened. But some of it came back in a hurry when he said, "That cop—Dan Sorenson. Now there's a guy with some solid meat to him. I told him so. Said my daughter could do a lot worse than him."

"You said what?" she cried, horrified.

"He's a hundred times the man that jerk you were engaged to was."

She groaned. "You can't mean you hinted Dan should marry me."

"No, I didn't come right out and say it. But he knew what I meant, all right. He's a canny one, that Dan."

She bit back angry words with difficulty, but couldn't help saying, "I thought you were going to try not to interfere in my life again."

"Who's interfering?" he asked. "I was just pointing out some home truths."

She sighed. Her father would never learn. "Please don't say anything like that to Dan again."

"Okay, okay. I'll call you again soon."

Home truths? The truth was her father might never stop interfering in her life. Could she reconcile with him knowing that? Her dad had always said what he thought and always would. But what on earth must Dan think?

Dan didn't call that evening, either, or Thursday or Friday. Friday evening her father phoned, thanked her again for getting back to him on Wednesday and asked if she could come over Saturday for lunch.

Oh, oh, here it comes, she thought. He was going to spring Nell on her.

"I'm not sure," she said cautiously. "I'll have to get back to you. And, remember if I do come, I'll be bringing the baby."

"Of course," he said. "I want Nell to see my cute little granddaughter."

Aha, it was out. "So she'll be there."

"Actually she's making the lunch. Nell's a great cook. She really would like to meet you."

Fay took a deep breath. Face it, she had to meet Nell sometime. But so soon? Before she was even sure she'd forgiven her father? "What time would it be, in case I can make it?"

"Around noon."

Well, it would give her somewhere to go tomorrow, Fay thought as she hung up. Now that she realized what her father had said to Dan, she no longer was surprised at his failure to call her, though it did hurt that he could make love to her so sweetly and then drop her. She sighed. To a man who'd vowed never to venture into marriage again, her father's words must have sounded as though he'd be getting his shotgun out next.

That evening she decided to bite the bullet and

meet Nell, since she really didn't want to go through the rest of her life at odds with her father. Besides, Danny Marie needed a grandfather. Calling her father back, Fay told him they would be there for lunch tomorrow.

The next day, Fay arrived at her father's house, her old childhood home, shortly after twelve. He was out the door almost before she had the ignition shut off.

"Let me carry my granddaughter in," he said after greeting her. "You don't need to bring that baby bed in, I brought your old crib down from the attic. Cleaned it up a bit and it's as good as new."

"I didn't know you'd kept my crib all those years," she told him as they walked toward the house.

"Forgot about it 'til Nell asked if I had anything to put the baby in. Fits real nice into the old sewing room."

Nell was waiting in the entry. She had short, curly gray hair, a pleasant face and a welcoming smile. "I'm so happy to meet you at last, Fay," she said. "I'm a hugger, so I hope you don't mind." She held out her arms.

Fay found she didn't mind too much being hugged by Nell. Her father beamed at them both, obviously pleased the initial meeting was going well.

"So this is your little one," Nell said, turning her attention to the baby. "Goodness, Hank, she's got your eyes." She looked at Fay. "Do you mind if I hold her?"

"Not at all." Which was the truth. Her first impression of Nell was that her father's choice was as open and honest as he was.

The baby smiled at Nell, pleasing everyone. After a few minutes spent admiring the baby, Nell handed her back to Hank. "You have a wonderful little daughter," she told Fay. "Your father is very lucky to be gifted with a granddaughter like her. Now, why don't you two sit down? I have a few last-minute things to do in the kitchen."

"I'll help." Fay offered.

Nell shook her head. "Thanks, but that's not necessary."

Still holding Danny Marie, Hank was already in what Fay knew he called his "easy chair." As she headed for the couch the doorbell rang.

"Get that, will you, honey?" Hank asked.

When Fay opened the door, Dan grinned down at her, sending her pulses pounding.

"Made it," he said. "Wasn't sure I could. Nice of your dad to invite me."

Speechless, she stood aside so he could enter. Nell came in from the kitchen for the introduction, greeted Dan and vanished once more.

Hank held up the baby, saying, "Your turn to take her, Dan. I think her diaper needs changing."

Fay, diaper bag in hand, led Dan to a small room off the hall where her mother had once kept her sewing machine. The old machine was still there, out of sight in its cabinet. The table where her mother once pinned patterns to material had been padded with a quilt so it could be used to change the baby's diaper. Since her father would never have thought of it, Fay knew Nell must have. There was also a step-on garbage pail under the table. Nell again.

"I can change her," she told Dan.

"You're surprised to see me," he said, laying the

baby atop the table, with a hand on her tummy, holding her there.

"My father didn't hand out an invitation list ahead of time."

"I gathered that." As he spoke he began to remove the dirty diaper.

Fay handed him a baby wipe. She took the folded diaper he handed her and deposited it in the pail, then gave him a clean one. Though she'd promised herself she absolutely wouldn't ask the burning question, she found it impossible to hold her tongue. "You didn't call."

"Got a new case that may be related to the one that sent me on administrative leave. If so, it'll be a tough nut to crack. Kept me so busy I couldn't get away. Anyway, I thought we both needed time." He secured the new diaper and lifted the baby into his arms, saying, "That better, Marie?"

Time to what? Decide never to see each other again? Which might not be a bad idea. Except now it was too late, as far as she was concerned. What was between them needed to run its course to get him out of her system once and for all.

She couldn't think of anything else to say except, "I see." To her horror, she found herself adding, "I suspected my father had scared you off."

"I don't scare easy."

An answer of sorts. And the only one she was going to get, apparently.

"Think she'll go to sleep if I put her in the crib and jiggle it a little?" he asked.

"Maybe. She's been fed."

Dan laid the baby in the crib, covering her with a blanket that looked new. "Time to close those big blue eyes, Marie,'' he crooned as he eased the crib back and forth gently on its rollers. He glanced at Fay. ''Know any lullabies? I have a limited repertoire.''

Since Danny Marie probably wouldn't go to sleep if they stood here talking over her head, Fay put the chance for a private conversation with Dan aside. She gazed down at her daughter and began to sing softly, ''Bye low, my baby, bye low, my pretty baby girl,'' She repeated the words three times, then hummed the tune until Danny Marie's eyes drooped shut.

They eased from the room.

''One your mother sang to you?'' Dan asked in a low tone as they approached the living room.

''My dad, actually. I don't remember, but Mom said he used to sing to me and she taught me the words.''

Strange, Fay had forgotten about that until just now.

''You're just in time,'' Nell announced from the kitchen archway. ''Lunch is served.''

Nell *was* a good cook, Fay realized as she sampled the food. It was too bad she simply didn't feel like eating. No doubt due to Dan's presence and his comment about them both needing time. She couldn't wait to hear his explanation.

They'd fallen into bed together. Both of them had enjoyed the experience. Neither expected anything permanent to come of it. Was it what her father had said, despite Dan insisting he didn't scare easy? He certainly couldn't have liked the comment. But if that was the problem, then why had he accepted Dad's invitation today?

After they'd all finished dessert and coffee, her father rose. ''I have an announcement to make. First, though, I want to thank Nell for a delicious meal. Her blueberry pie rivals any I've tasted.''

He allowed Fay and Dan to add their compliments to the cook, then cleared his throat. ''I've finally persuaded Nell to set a wedding date. We'll be married on August 15. Nothing fancy, just a small reception following the church ceremony. You'll both be getting your wedding invitations soon, but I wanted you to know ahead of time.'' His gaze settled on Fay. ''I hope you'll be happy for us.''

She swallowed, stunned. Pulling herself together, she rose and managed to say, ''Of course.''

Nell jumped up, hurried over and threw her arms around Fay. ''Thank you, my dear. Thank you so much.'' When she pulled away, Fay noticed tears running down her cheeks.

Nell hadn't thought she would approve, she realized, feeling guilty for all the negative thoughts she'd had about her father's companion before meeting her. *Do I really approve?* she asked herself. The happy smile on her father's face touched her heart.

This was the man who'd sung lullabies to his pretty baby girl, who'd pushed her on park swings, who'd taught her how to catch a ball and row a boat. Who'd read the comics to her before she'd learned to read them herself and who taught her how to deal with bullies.

Interfering as he was, he loved her, had always loved her. Swallowing to rid herself of the lump in her throat, she offered her father a genuine smile. How could she not be happy for him?

Fay listened bemusedly to Dan congratulate her father and then watched him give Nell a hug. ''I had no idea I was invited to an engagement lunch,'' he told her. ''Best one I ever ate.''

Nell beamed at him.

Hearing a tentative wail from the other room, Fay breathed a sigh of relief. She needed an excuse to get away for a bit and get over her shock, and also the feeling that she might burst into tears. Never once had she suspected her father meant to marry his companion. Foolish of her. Her father was the marrying sort. Unlike Dan. Or her.

''I must see to the baby,'' she said and left the kitchen.

She was sitting in the sewing room rocking chair nursing Danny Marie, when Dan edged around the door she'd left ajar. ''I can't stay,'' he told her. ''I'll finish up what I have to do and then stop by your place later.''

Just like that. Assuming she wanted him to. Not even asking if it was okay. Men were like that, why should she expect him to be any different? Even if he was.

''We do need to talk,'' she muttered finally.

He grinned. ''That, too. See you as soon as I can make it.'' And then he was gone.

''You may as well learn early, little one,'' she murmured to the baby, ''that men are not to be trusted.''

Yes, and also that, difficult as it sometimes was to get along with them, it was impossible to get along without them.

It wasn't until she was ready to bring Danny Marie out to socialize with her father and Nell that the import of what Dan had told her about the new case hit home. If this was connected to the one where he'd got shot, didn't that mean it'd be dangerous? She controlled her instinctive shiver of fear for him. Dan was a detective, a cop. For all she knew, he was always in danger.

For some reason that had never really come home to her despite all he'd told her about his ex-wife's fears. Yet he liked what he did, despite the danger. If he didn't worry about it, she'd try not to. Because worry was a useless emotion.

"Dan'll be safe," she whispered to the baby. "I know he will."

At that moment she realized how much he meant to her and that scared her more than any fear he might be in danger.

Chapter Twelve

Back at her apartment, Fay changed Danny Marie, while talking to her as if she were her best friend. "The trouble is I want to see Dan. And, blast the man, he's right—not just to talk. I can't seem to get him out of my mind. He's lodged there now, even though what I want to think about is how to come to terms with my father marrying Nell."

Before Fay had left her dad's house, he'd confided that he was selling it and Nell was also selling the house she'd lived in with her husband. "There's no use burdening a new marriage with old memories, even though they may be good ones." Hank had said. "We're going to start out with a place that's ours, Nell's and mine."

"That sounds like a good idea," Fay had said, and meant it. It would help her, too. This way, she wouldn't have to visit and see Nell in the house that had been her mother's.

It hadn't occurred to her until this minute that Nell's daughter—what was her name?—might also feel better if Hank Merriweather wasn't living in her father's house. Aware she'd be meeting the girl at the wedding, Fay searched for the name, recalling it was a combination of the father and mother's names. Oh yes, Jonell, called Jo.

Good grief, the marriage would mean she was acquiring a stepsister!

"That means you'll have an Aunt Jo," she told the baby.

After Danny Marie settled down to sleep, Fay threw in a load of wash and emptied the garbage and trash cans into the large container out in back. No way did she intend to sit around twiddling her thumbs to wait for any man's arrival, and that included Dan. When she finally ran out of chores, she opened her briefcase, sat down and studied the printouts from work. She might be good, but only fools didn't check for errors.

To her extreme annoyance, she found she couldn't concentrate on the papers in front of her. Maybe if she used the computer she could. She turned it on and remembered there'd been something she wanted to look up on the Internet. After she'd stuck the info she needed into a temporary file folder, she wondered if any of the Sorensons had ever tried to find their mother via the Net. Megan had given her an e-mail address. Should she e-mail Megan to let her know if she ever wanted to search for her mother, the Internet would be the place to begin?

Fay shook her head. She'd already learned not to

mention his mother to Dan. It really was none of her business and might only upset Megan.

Pushing everything else firmly from her mind, Fay forced herself to concentrate on checking through her work project, which was going well. Why, then, did she wish she was nearer to finishing it? She'd known when she took it on that the job would take over a month, maybe two.

The baby woke. Fay fed her again, bathed her, played with her and settled Danny Marie in her crib. Not feeling especially hungry after the big lunch, Fay made popcorn and ate it with chocolate milk, one of her favorite treats. As she cleaned the kitchen, she tried to decide what do when Dan showed up. Once he kissed her could she hang on to any plan other than to let nature take its course? Probably not, but she could at least straighten him out about how she felt concerning her father's remark. And pry out of him why he'd thought they needed time to sort things out after last Tuesday.

The door chime startled her. From the living room window, she saw Dan's car parked under the streetlight. Still, at the door she checked to see that the chain was on, then asked, "Who is it?"

"Dan."

She slid the door open the few inches the chain allowed. Dan, without a doubt. Closing the door, she slipped off the chain and opened it again. "Does my performance meet with your approval, Sergeant Sorenson?" she asked as he stepped inside.

He frowned.

"No levity allowed where safety is concerned?" she teased.

"You got that right." He didn't smile as he said it.

Maybe cops tended to be paranoid about safety. She dropped the subject. "Want anything?" she asked.

That earned her a grin. "What do you think?"

"I meant to eat or drink."

"Nothing like that."

"I thought we were going to talk. You need to explain what you meant about us needing time."

He sighed. "Never met such a woman for nailing every comment to the wall."

"Come into the living room where we can be comfortable."

"On the couch," he suggested.

She raised her eyebrows. "If you promise to explain before getting too 'comfortable.'"

He put a hand over his heart as he followed her into the room. "Your wish is my command."

"Why don't I believe that?"

Dan settled himself on the couch. "Because your father raised you to know better?"

She eased down near him, but not touching. "That's another thing. No matter what my father may think or say, you know perfectly well I have no intention of marrying you—or any man."

He nodded. "Since marriage isn't in the picture for either of us, that's why I figured we needed a little time to get used to what's between us."

"Which is?"

"You define it. With no 'ums.'"

She started to say lust, then didn't. Her feelings for him were more complicated than pure lust. "I can't define it," she said finally. "I guess we've invented an inexplicable relationship."

"So you don't have an answer either." He reached over and pulled her close to him. "Since neither of us has, let's get comfortable."

"Without knowing why?" She heard the breathlessness in her voice, induced by his hand caressing the nape of her neck.

"I'd rather think about how. I saw baby powder in the nursery. Make you think of anything other than powdering the baby's bottom?"

"I don't use the powder—it was a gift."

"I've got another use for it. Back rub."

"I thought lotion was the usual method."

"Both work. Especially if the first requirement of getting naked is met."

"I thought you only needed a bare back."

"Tunnel vision." He rose, pulled her up off the couch and led her into the bedroom. "Tonight we get undressed first. Not in the middle of action."

"You first."

"Okay." He reached out and pulled her shirt over her head.

"I didn't mean we'd undress each other," she sputtered.

"But I did."

Hesitantly she reached for the buttons on his shirt and undid them. She'd never actually undressed a man before and, as she slid the shirt off his arms she found it surprisingly arousing.

He backed her against the bed until she sat on it, then got down on one knee and removed her sandals.

"Shoes it is," she murmured. He obediently sat and she crouched to remove his shoes and socks. His feet were longer and wider than hers, powerful-looking, just like his hands. She could hardly wait to have those hands touching her.

"Before we go any further, I'll liberate the powder," he told her. "Just in case we get distracted later on."

She was already distracted and took several deep and calming breaths while he collected the powder from the nursery and set the can on the bedside table.

"A man's dream, the front-opening bra," he said, releasing the clasp and easing it off her shoulders. He shook his head. "No, this man's dream is what I see now that the bra is gone."

A sizzle shot along her nerves at the look in his eyes. She swallowed. "No undershirt, so I guess..." Her words trailed off as she unfastened his belt and unhooked the fastener at the top of his pants. Her fingers trembled as she found the zipper and slid it slowly and carefully over his obvious arousal before pushing the pants down so they fell around his ankles. He stepped out of them, kicking them aside.

He unbuttoned her skirt at the side opening and slid the zipper down, allowing the skirt to puddle at her feet.

She took great care to lower his undershorts past his arousal. Down they went, leaving him naked.

"Oh, my," she said involuntarily. She definitely liked what she saw.

He slipped a finger under the elastic band of her bikinis and pulled them down to the floor. She stepped free of them and stood before him, heart pounding at the admiration in his gaze.

"Good thing I got the powder when I did," he said huskily. "It sure would be too late now. Going to be too late anyway, if you don't get facedown on that bed in a hurry.''

She pulled the covers back to the foot of the bed and lay down. He sat beside her and she felt him sprinkle powder onto the small of her back, its faintly flowery scent drifting to her nostrils. And then his hands touched her, spreading the powder up her spine, down her sides, pausing to caress what he could reach of her breasts. When he came to the small of her back again, he ran his hands over the curves of her rear and down her legs to her heels.

She could feel herself dissolve as he started back up, her insides pure liquid, the touch of his hands sending erotic messages to every cell in her body.

Over and over he caressed her until, wanting to make him as helplessly aroused as she was, she murmured, ''My turn now.''

Instead of lying face-down, he turned sideways. She had to clear her throat before she was able to speak, even then her voice was husky. ''Aren't you supposed to be on your stomach?''

''Got a problem with that,'' he told her. She smiled, realizing why.

She poured powder onto her hands and knelt beside him on the bed, doing her best to reach all of his back. Running her hands over his bare flesh was every bit as arousing as having him touch her. How much more of this teasing could she stand? As much as he could, anyway. She slid her hands over his butt and on down to his heels, then up his back again, repeating the movements until the last time, when she let her hands linger on his butt, then deliberately allowed them to wander on the way back up, brushing his arousal.

He flung himself onto his back and pulled her over him.

"I was just getting started," she murmured, as she rearranged herself so his arousal was between her legs.

"Stop wiggling or we'll be in trouble," he told her.

She reached her hand down to guide him as she raised herself up so he could slide inside. She tried to tease him by drawing back, then easing down, but her own need compelled her to let him thrust deeply again and again. Holding her to him, he turned them both onto their sides, then over until he was on top. His mouth covered hers in a kiss so passionate she felt she was on fire, burning with need.

"Fay," he whispered. "My beautiful Fay."

As if his words were the trigger, she reached the peak, crying out with release, hearing his cry echo hers. He held her close until they were all the way down, then turned them both onto their sides.

When she felt able to talk, she started to tell him that was the most fantastic back rub anyone ever had, then heard his deep breathing and realized he'd fallen asleep. At the same time she heard Danny Marie begin to fuss.

Fay eased herself from his arms, found a robe and went to her daughter. "What a good sense of timing you have," she murmured as she picked up the baby, changed her, then used a wipe to clean herself before she sat down to nurse her daughter.

She thought about Dan sleeping in her bed. He would be the first man to stay overnight if she decided to allow that. Ken had been angry about her rule, but she'd held to it. The rule, she'd decided long ago, was part of being an only child. She'd always slept alone. Slumber parties with other girls didn't count because everyone brought a sleeping bag and you were alone in it. As far as actually sleeping was concerned, she just didn't feel right with anyone in her bed.

What about Dan? She sighed. After all, in the cabin hadn't she slept many nights in the same room with him? What was so different about this?

Him being in her bed with her was the difference.

She finished nursing the baby and rocked her until Danny Marie fell asleep again, then laid her in the crib, all the time wondering how she was going to tell Dan about her rule. She hadn't come to any decision by the time she took off her robe and slid back into her bed. Because she couldn't bear to wake him up, she turned her back to him, prepared to wait to say anything until he roused by himself. He mumbled something unintelligible, rolled over and drew her close so they lay spoon fashion, her back to his front, his arm draped over her. She found herself relaxing as she relished the feeling of coziness.

After a time his arm tightened its hold, he pulled her closer until her rear pressed his arousal. Involuntarily, she wiggled her butt against him.

"Mmm," he murmured sleepily, turning her to face him. "Nice surprise. Thought I was dreaming."

His kiss was languorous, drawing her into an invitation to passion. His hands, caressing her body, moved slowly, finding new places to explore. In turn, she searched out corresponding sites on him, enjoying the sensation of his bare skin under her fingers.

"You feel so good," she murmured against his lips.

"Touching you is addictive," he whispered in her ear. "I'm hooked."

Their lips met again, the kiss deepening. She would know Dan's taste anywhere, a taste that belonged to him alone and one she couldn't get enough of.

Dan breathed in Fay's own special scent, spicier than roses. With her in his arms he had everything he wanted. Which scared the hell out of him sometimes. At the moment, though, nothing else mattered but making love with her.

He'd always tried to satisfy the woman he was with, but she was special. Her satisfaction was more important to him than his own climax. Maybe that was why every time with her was so good. Better than with any other woman. But then his stubborn, risk-taking Fay wasn't like any other woman.

His? For now, yes. For this moment when she trembled in his embrace, ready for him, wanting what he wanted.

She made the world go away when she welcomed him inside her. His mind blanked into pure sensation as they danced the lovemaking waltz together.

Afterward he longed to stay in her bed, holding her in his arms while they fell asleep. But falling asleep here was exactly what he couldn't do. To be with her, he'd already taken too much time away from the case he was working on. He needed to check out that Huron Street tavern before it closed for the night.

Leaning to Fay, he kissed her quickly. "I can't stay," he told her. "I already played truant to be with you."

"The new case?"

"Right." He rolled out of bed, fumbling on the

floor for his scattered clothes by the meager illumination of the night-light.

"Um, I was just going to mention that I'd rather you didn't sleep over," she said as he dressed hurriedly.

He paused for a moment. Um? That meant she wasn't telling the whole story. At the same time he felt a flare of annoyance. She didn't want him sleeping in her bed? It made him feel like some guy she'd picked up in a bar.

"Worried about the neighbors?" he asked.

"Not exactly."

There was no time to get into it. "I've got to hightail it," he told her. "Don't forget to put the chain back on."

As he pulled away in his car, he tried to clear his mind so he could focus on what he needed to be doing. Nothing in his life had ever distracted him from work, but he wasn't so sure she wouldn't prove to be the exception.

Sunday didn't turn out to be Fay's favorite day. She'd had trouble getting back to sleep after she'd put the blasted chain back on and that, combined with the sleep she hadn't gotten for other reasons, made her edgy. Danny Marie, ordinarily the most amiable of babies fussed off and on for most of the day. When taking her temperature showed she had no fever, Fay couldn't understand what was wrong. Finally she called Clara.

"How's your cold?" she asked.

"Better, dear. I think I can take care of the baby on Wednesday."

"That's good news, but she's been fussy all day. No fever. I'm worried."

"Are her gums red and swollen?" Clara asked

"I don't know. I didn't look."

"She could be cutting a tooth. Do you have a teething ring?"

"I think somebody gave me one."

"Put it in the freezer for a bit until it gets cold, then let her chew on it. Sometimes the cold helps."

Clara's diagnosis turned out to be spot on and her suggestion for treatment did help. But Danny Marie was far from her usual happy self. Fay worried about having to leave her with Yvonne in the morning. For the first time she could recall, she resented the fact she had to go to work. Her client, though, would be back from New York and would want her input on what had gone on there.

She'd thought Dan might call, but she supposed she ought to get used to the fact he was working on a case. She wondered if her telling him she didn't want him spending the night in her bed had bothered him. Too bad if it did. On her turf, they played by her rules.

The strange thing was that she almost hadn't told him her rule. Not until he'd said he had to go. Why was it they so often seemed on the verge of a disagreement? Was it because neither of them was quite sure just where they were headed with each other?

When the phone finally rang, she hurried to answer it.

"Oh, hello, Dad," she said hoping she didn't sound disappointed because the call hadn't been from Dan.

"Thanks for coming by for lunch yesterday," he said. "Nell was so pleased you could make it."

"I enjoyed meeting her," Fay said truthfully, juggling the baby from one arm to the other.

"I can hear the baby fussing. Is she sick?"

Without warning, Fay burst into tears, surprising her and alarming her father. When she finally was able to speak, she assured her father the baby was all right, just cutting a tooth.

"Sounds like you're not all right, though," he said. "I think Nell and I better come over."

"No, no," she protested. "I don't—" But she was too late, he'd already hung up.

That was all she needed. A fussy baby, a father she'd barely forgiven and a step-mother-to-be she hardly knew.

When they rang the bell twenty minutes later, still holding Danny Marie, she remembered to use the chain.

After her father was inside, he said. "You didn't used to have a chain. Bet it was Dan's idea. It's a good safety measure."

Fay gritted her teeth. "Please don't go on about Dan," she said.

"What's the matter? You two have a spat?"

She shook her head, not wanting to blow up at him, but feeling she was going to.

"Don't make Fay feel worse," Nell put in. "A fussy baby is more than enough to frazzle any mother." She glanced at Fay as if to say, *men*.

"Let me take the baby," Nell said.

Fay handed over Danny Marie without hesitation, relieved to have the older woman look after her for a bit. She'd moved the cradle back into the living room and Nell spotted it as she sat in a nearby chair. "What a lovely old cradle. You can tell it was hand-crafted. Your work, Hank?"

He shook his head. "I'm not up to fancy carpentry like that."

"It came from Dan's family," Fay said, reluctantly. Heaven only knew what her father might read into that. "Can I get you anything?"

"No, thanks." Nell and her father spoke as one.

"We stopped at the drug store," Nell added, "and bought something to soothe the poor little baby's gums. It's perfectly harmless." She looked from the baby to Nell. "I don't believe I ever did hear your daughter's real name."

Fay had known this moment would come, so had prepared herself. "Her name is Danielle Marie, I call her Danny Marie. But Dan doesn't know I named her after him. Actually, he thinks her name is Marie, but he always calls her Peanut. I'd rather he didn't find out."

Her father gave her an odd look. "I think Dan would be proud you named your baby after him."

"Dad, I just told you—"

"Your father won't mention it to Dan and neither will I," Nell said soothingly. "Will we, Hank?"

"No, no, of course not."

"Now, let's try out these drops to rub on the baby's gums," Nell said. "Give her the bottle, Hank."

Fay took it from her father and read the ingredients, which seemed harmless enough, then the directions.

"I'll hold her while you rub the magic potion on," Nell said.

"I hope it *is* magic," Fay told her. "She's usually

such a good baby. The way she's acting I can tell she's in real distress and I feel so helpless.''

"That's what we mothers all have to go through," Nell agreed.

"Fathers, too," Hank said. "I nearly went out of my mind that night when you weren't yet two and had croup so bad. Finally I remembered an old remedy of my grandmother's. You and I spent hours on a kitchen chair near the stove with pans of water boiling on all the burners. We steamed up the whole room before your breathing eased and you fell asleep in my arms."

All of Fay's irritation with her father dissipated as she listened to a part of her growing up that she'd known nothing about.

"I was never so glad to see my pretty little baby sleep as I was then," he added. "Never forgot it."

Pretty little baby. From the lullaby she sang to Danny Marie. The same one her father had sung to her.

Blinking back tears, Fay managed to rub some of the liquid on her baby's swollen gum. While she was doing it, her father picked up the cradle and brought it close to a chair.

Easing down into the chair, he said, "Put Danny Marie in the cradle and I'll rock her with my foot 'til she falls asleep."

"That really is a lovely name," Nell put in as she placed the baby in the cradle. Looking at Fay, she said, "Do you mind if I make myself at home in your kitchen and fix a cup of tea for us all? I find tea soothing."

When Fay made a move to go with her, Nell waved

her back down. "No, no, you stay and watch the baby."

"She's even gotten me to drink tea now," Hank said after Nell disappeared into the kitchen. "Less caffeine than coffee, she claims. Better for my blood pressure."

Fay gave him a wan smile. Danny Marie was making little sucking noises, as though tasting what was on her lower gum, but she actually seemed to be settling down. When it looked as though the baby was going to sleep, Fay started to relax and realized this was her chance to tackle her father.

"Dad," she said, "promise me you won't ever mention marriage or even hint about it to Dan again."

"Why would I want to do that?"

"Don't play innocent. You're my father, that's why. Promise me."

"I'll promise, if you'll promise me not to choose another Ken."

"That's one mistake I'm not likely to make again. But I want you to know I don't have any intention of marrying Dan. Or any other man."

He sighed. "That's a real shame."

"Maybe. But it's my life."

"I won't meddle," he promised. "I just want to see you happy. Never expected to be again myself. I loved your mother and Nell loved Joe. We were both surprised when we found we could make each other happy."

Though Fay didn't reply, she was glad Nell had come along for her father. She was also glad he'd told her about how he'd cared for little Fay when she was sick, because it made her better able to understand why he hadn't wanted her to carry her pregnancy to term. He'd been worried about her and felt helpless to fix everything the way he had when she was a child.

She smiled at him. "It's okay, Dad. I am happy."

Later, after they'd left, Fay left the sleeping baby where she was in the cradle and went in the bedroom to get herself ready for bed. Early as it was, she felt exhausted.

With more exposure to Nell, she'd begun to realize her father had found a treasure. Nell was a kind and thoughtful woman who really cared about the man she was going to marry.

The phone rang.

"How's Peanut?" Dan asked. "Is she better?"

So much for her father not meddling, Fay told herself. How else would Dan have known about the baby?

"She's asleep. Nell's gum medicine worked."

"That's good to hear. Let me know if anything serious happens."

She heard voices in the background, then the thin wail of a siren. "Something's going down," he said. "No more time to talk."

There was no chance to get even a word in before he was gone. He might have been busy, she told herself, but, if he cared, he could have taken an extra two seconds to ask if she was okay.

It certainly showed who mattered the most to him.

Chapter Thirteen

Before she left for work the next morning, Fay discovered the top of a tooth was poking through after running her finger over Danny Marie's sore gum. The baby seemed in much less distress, which made it a bit easier to leave her with Yvonne. Nell and her father had also promised to come by and check on her.

At work, she discovered she'd been right about her client wanting to discuss the New York trip with her. In fact, on his next trip, scheduled for the last week in August, he wanted her to accompany him. Since his wife would also be along because she loved shopping in Manhattan, Fay had no problem with that aspect of the trip. But she cringed at the idea of being so far from her baby for three and a half days.

She'd discussed switching from breast-feeding to a formula for Danny Marie with her doctor, who'd indicated it was up to her if she wished to. Actually she did and, if she decided to make the trip to New York, maybe trying the switch a week or so before would help. But what if something happened to her daughter while she was away? True, Clara was trustworthy, plus her father and Nell would be there to take care of any emergency. Danny Marie was so little, though—never mind how healthy the pediatrician said she was.

She finally told her client she would get back to him about the trip. How was it she'd ever believed returning to work would be a simple matter of finding a reliable baby-sitter? Leaving her baby with someone else, no matter how reliable, was far more difficult than she'd realized. Getting ahead and staying there might be important, but, Fay decided, having a baby skewed her former parameters.

At the end of her day, on the drive home, for the first time in her life, she found herself questioning the precepts her mother had always stressed. "To get ahead, you must set goals, work hard, always do your best. Never let it be said you didn't become all you could have been."

Though her mother had never actually said it in so many words, the implication had always been there that Hank Merriweather had failed to live up to these expectations. For some reason, until this moment, it had never occurred to Fay that her mother's expectations about her father came from a woman who'd never worked outside the home. She'd seemed content to be a housewife, though she did do alterations and make beautifully designed clothes for selected customers.

Was that her mother's best? The question disturbed

Fay, making her wonder if she'd been chosen as a substitute to reach goals her mother had never striven for.

Never mind that she was proud of her accomplishments, did she still believe getting ahead was the most important thing in life?

"I loved my mother," she said aloud. Hearing her own words made her realize she'd always loved her father, too, even if she'd believed he didn't have enough drive.

She still loved him. He'd been wrong to hurt her the way he had, but he'd realized that and had told her he was sorry.

Was it possible she'd been wrong, too, in thinking he lacked ambition? After all, he'd risen from an entry-level job at the foundry to become the foreman.

Fay arrived home shaken by this new direction her thoughts had taken. She came into the apartment to find Yvonne gone and her father and Nell with the baby.

"What's wrong?" she cried, panicking.

"Calm down, nothing to worry about," her dad said.

"It looks like Danny Marie's cutting another tooth," Nell added. "When we came by, Mrs. Tousignant was at her wit's end trying to pacify the baby, so we told her we'd take over until you got home. I hope that was all right?"

Fay nodded, reassured by the sight of her daughter sleeping in the cradle by the chair her father sat in, one of his feet on the rocker.

"Thank heaven I don't have to work tomorrow," she said.

By Wednesday the other tooth had broken through and Danny Marie's sunny nature resurfaced. Clara, over her sniffles, came to take care of her, so Fay set off, telling herself all was well. Still, a niggling doubt remained and "what ifs?" poked their ugly heads up all through her workday.

Her worry was for nothing. Her daughter remained well.

On Thursday, Fay caught up on all the chores she hadn't gotten to on Tuesday. In the back of her mind she'd kept expecting Dan to call. He didn't, and she began wondering if her dad was keeping him posted about the baby. Even if that was true, though, he still could have called to talk to her.

Friday zipped by and gave way to Saturday, when it rained, keeping Fay from taking a walk with the baby. Despite the extra work she'd brought home, the day dragged. Sunday Clara invited her for lunch.

"I wanted to ask your young man, too, but I couldn't reach him," Clara said.

"You mean he wasn't home?"

"I left a message on his answering machine, but he didn't get back to me. Is he out of town?"

"I don't know."

"He's such a fine man," Clara said. "I hope you don't mind my saying so, but he's head and shoulders above poor Ken."

Fay managed to make a sound of agreement. Clara meant well and she wouldn't dream of being cross with her. But when she hung up, Fay thought bitterly that Dan could have taken a trip to Mars for all she knew. Or he just might figure a message left by Clara meant he'd have to see Fay Merriweather and so didn't call back.

Face it, she told herself, he doesn't care. She hadn't

believed he was like so many men who pursued a
woman until they got her in bed and then lost interest.
But what else was she supposed to think? True, he
had a new case, a tough one by the sound of it, but
did that make him too busy, day and night, seven days
a week to pick up a phone and say hello?

Of course, despite Dan's denials, it was possible
her father's hints about marriage had scared him off.

If that's true, she told herself, *then he's not likely
to show up for the wedding on the fifteenth, and I can
stop worrying over where the blasted relationship is
headed because I'll never see him again.*

Sunday evening, Dan paced back and forth in his
crummy downtown hotel room, lonely as hell. He'd
never minded undercover work before because he
hadn't had to do much to change his appearance. This
time the chief had thought Dan's face was too well
known because of the "hero" coverage, so he had
Dan dye his hair a dark blue, stop shaving and then
get one ear pierced so he could wear an earring. Add
cheap mod clothes, a slouch hat and presto—scumbag
Lon Kingery emerged.

Dan hardly recognized his image in the mirror as
himself. He was sure even his partner Gary would
never give Lon a second look if he passed him on the
street. Great disguise, but he really hated the dangling
gold earring. He figured once he came out of cover,
somehow the guys would hear about the damn earring
and razz the hell out of him.

It turned out this case *was* related to the other,
where he killed who they believed was the head hon-
cho, the guy that had shot him first. But the dead perp
had been one of two heads. The other was still at large

and still running drugs. Dan's job was to go under-cover to ID the guy and find out where he operated from. More or less a secret mission. No one was sup-posed to know.

Another good reason a cop shouldn't marry. Wives expected to be told where and why husbands were going to disappear for a couple of weeks. Hell, even if a guy was in any kind of a serious relationship, the woman expected to be told these things. He figured Fay would be teed off with him when he got back. Which would be barely in time for her dad's wedding.

On the other hand, this forced time undercover gave him time to think. The problem was, when you needed a particular woman in your arms, thinking didn't do zip. So his feelings for her were complicated enough to scare him at times. So what? He still wanted to be with her.

Sure, he could call her from somewhere around here, even if he wasn't supposed to, but if he wasn't going to tell her where he was or why, which she'd certainly want to know, what was the point?

He'd expected to locate the guy before the week-end, but that hadn't happened. He was close, but so far no cigar. Damn. Even that retro saying reminded him of Fay.

He stopped pacing and sat on the edge of the crummy bed, staring into space, wondering if Fay and Marie were okay. He'd never missed a woman so much in his life. As far as he was concerned, their affair could go on indefinitely.

Until she met someone else. Lots of high-powered types out there roaming around. Her type. Or at least she thought so. He gritted his teeth. Damn it, Fay was his.

Can it, Sorenson, he told himself. *That's anger thinking.*

* * *

Lon made the ID late Thursday night, managed to attach a tracer to the perp's car and then abandoned the dingy hotel room for Dan's apartment, his job done. Dan immediately tried to get rid of Lon. The supposedly not-permanent dark blue hair dye refused to wash out completely under the shower, rendering his hair a sort of pale blue mixed with blond, but he was able to shave and discard the earring. He checked the messages on his answering machine, finding an outdated one from Clara. None from Fay. Looking at his watch he decided it was too late to call Fay tonight.

The wedding was the next day and he'd be seeing her then, so he could explain what he'd been doing in person—better than a phone call any day. Face-to-face, she couldn't hang up on him.

Even though Fay didn't want to marry, it'd been his observation that women got all sentimental about weddings and he figured that'd be in his favor. Then, too, it wasn't really his fault he hadn't called her. His explanation was perfectly logical.

But, at St. Dunstan's Church the next afternoon, while the Merriweather-Yates wedding party was waiting for a previous wedding party to vacate the premises, Dan discovered the most logical explanation was useless if you couldn't corner the recipient to hear it. Fay, looking as lovely as he'd ever seen her in a filmy dress the color of birch leaves in the fall, seemed to have an uncanny ability to move somewhere else just as he zeroed in on her.

He finally caught up to her as they began to file

into the church. Holding her arm firmly, he muttered, "Stop trying to avoid me."

"Why would you think I'd do that?" Her voice was as chilly as a December north wind off Lake Superior.

"Because you are. You owe me the courtesy of listening to me."

"I owe you nothing." Her voice rose slightly, causing several of the guests to glance their way.

She bit her lip.

"I had to go undercover but couldn't tell you. It's part of my job," he said quickly.

"I don't care what—" She paused in midsentence, the meaning of his words evidently belatedly catching up to her, and looked hard at him.

"I guess that explains the blue hair," she said after a moment.

Deciding to ignore that, he said, "So I couldn't call or come to see you. Missed you, though."

"Oh."

"Finished the job late last night, too late to call you." His gaze checked her out from head to toe. "You look almost too good to take to bed."

Her lips twitched as though trying to hold back a smile. "Flattery will get you nowhere." To his relief, amusement and warmth replaced the chill in her voice.

"The dress you're wearing makes your eyes turn gold," he added. He kept to himself what he'd like to do with the dress—tear it off, along with the rest of her clothes and make love all this beautiful Saturday afternoon.

"Where's Peanut?" he asked instead.

"Clara's looking after her until the reception's over."

"Did the baby tooth come in okay?"

"She's cut two teeth."

"And I missed that."

"Among other things. You really were undercover?"

"If you think I dyed my hair blue because I wanted—"

He broke off as an usher asked, "Bride or groom?" Momentarily startled, he let Fay answer.

"Groom," Fay murmured, and the usher indicated which side of the church they were to sit on.

Dan made sure she got an aisle seat so she'd be able to see everything. Sitting next to her, he relaxed for the first time since arriving at St. Dunstan's. He was with Fay. Nothing else mattered. Noticing she was peering over at the bride's side of the church, he asked who she was looking for.

"Like you, Nell's daughter, Jo, didn't get in from Chicago until late last night," she said. "I haven't had a chance to meet her."

He'd forgotten Nell even had a daughter.

"Do you realize Jo's going to be my stepsister?"

He hadn't thought about that, either. All his focus had been on Fay.

The organist began playing a familiar melody, something he vaguely recalled from other weddings he'd been to. The minister appeared from a side entrance. Looking back, Dan saw Hank Merriweather leading his bride-to-be up the aisle.

"Nell looks so happy," Fay whispered. "Her silver-gray suit really suits her, don't you think?"

Dan supposed so. Hank looked more smug than

anything else. Probably because the man was well-satisfied in his choice of a bride. The groom was evidently as happy as the bride. Wasn't that how it was supposed to be?

Thinking back to his marriage to Jean, Dan remembered his nervousness on his wedding day. He watched the older couple take their place at the altar.

Fay sighed. "I'm glad they found each other. At first I was only thinking she was good for my father because she cared about him, but I've come to realize he's good for her, too, because he really does love her."

Fay noticed Dan shift restlessly. Was he bored? No, her glance at him showed her he looked more uneasy than anything else. She focused on the pair at the altar again. How handsome her father looked in his dark suit, his normally untidy fair hair smooth and neat. Dan's hair was almost the same color—or had been before the blue phase. Of course, Dan had all of his, while her father was slowly balding.

After her father and Nell had exchanged vows, Hank bent to kiss Nell and, all of a sudden Fay's perception shifted so that for a moment she saw not the older couple, but Fay and Dan standing at the altar, he leaning to kiss her. She shook her head, taking a deep breath. What was the matter with her? To her surprise, tears filled her eyes.

As she dabbed at the tears with a tissue, she heard Dan say, "Why is it women almost always cry at weddings?"

"Why do men get uneasy?" she snapped, angry at herself, but taking it out on him.

"I'm not uneasy. Just impatient to get you out of here and into—"

"Shh," she said, glancing at the couple next to them. "They're listening."

He shrugged. "You still haven't told me why women cry."

Fay thought frantically. Never would she reveal what she'd projected up there.

"Um, women often cry when they're happy. I'm happy for both my father and for Nell."

"Me, too. But I'm glad it's over. I suppose we have to stay for the wedding reception, though."

She wondered if he was remembering his own wedding—and its subsequent failure. "You know we do. So on to the reception."

But the thought of Dan maybe having had to relive his past troubled her. She'd felt bad enough having to tell Ken she couldn't marry him. How much worse it would have been to marry someone and then realize you shouldn't have.

Two flutes of champagne banished her temporary depression. Next to the bridal couple she spotted a young woman who, from her resemblance to Nell, must be Jo. She introduced herself and Dan.

Glasses covered Jo's beautiful green eyes. Fay classified her looks as about average until she smiled and her whole face lit up.

"What a marvelous smile you have," she said.

"Thanks. People often mention that," Jo said, "so I figure it must be my best feature. The trouble comes when I don't feel like smiling. There I am, deprived of my best feature."

Dan grinned at Jo. "Think of it this way. Without your dazzling smile to distract them, people can begin to appreciate the rest of you."

As Fay watched Jo respond to the compliment, she

felt a sudden heaviness in her chest. Was he attracted to Jo? Almost immediately she was ashamed of herself. Dan was just being friendly. Wasn't he?

The band started playing, the music from her father and Nell's era, and Dan whirled her off to dance. Once again in his arms, where she belonged, Fay forgot about Jo. "Think they'll play a waltz?" she asked.

"I hate to think of what might happen if they do."

Into the next number, though, she began to regret the second flute of champagne. She'd never been much of a drinker and, apparently, two was one too many for her. Her discomfort grew until she excused herself to go to the ladies' room and bolted from the dance floor. She made it just in time and promptly threw up. Not long after, feeling somewhat better, she washed her face, applied new makeup and went back to the party.

She smiled as she spotted her father and Nell dancing while they gazed into each other's eyes. An older man, Oscar Miles, she'd been introduced to earlier, came up and asked her to dance. Since she hadn't yet located Dan, she agreed, not wanting to seem stand-offish at her father's wedding reception.

Oscar proved to be a Fred Astaire wannabe and she found it hard to keep up with his intricate and fancy steps. During a particularly difficult sequence, she happened to notice Dan dancing with Jo, both of them laughing, apparently intent on each other. Her concentration broken, she stumbled, slipped and started to fall. Oscar's quick grab saved her, but in the process she twisted her ankle and he had to help her off the floor.

He led her to a chair and found a footstool for her

to rest her injured leg on. "Shall I call someone?" he asked.

"No, no, I'll be fine," she assured him. He kept hovering over her until she said, "Really, I'm okay, I just need to rest for a bit." She managed a smile and made a shooing motion with her hand. "You don't need to stay with me."

He finally left her alone. She sat there, her ankle throbbing, feeling sorry for herself and angry at Dan. She wouldn't have stumbled if she hadn't seen him so cozy with Jo. After a time, she recognized what she was feeling. Good grief—jealousy. Fay Merriweather, who had never cared enough about any man to be jealous, was jealous.

Eventually her father and Nell found her. Looking at her ankle, now somewhat swollen, Nell said, "Goodness, that must hurt. Would you like us to take you to the emergency room?"

Fay shook her head. "I twisted my ankle, but I'm sure I didn't break anything. I've got one of those elastic bandages at home. If I put ice on it and then the bandage, I'll be all right."

"Then we'll take you home."

"And miss your own reception? Certainly not."

"I'll get Dan to do the honors," her father said.

"Oh, no, I—" Fay began, but her father was already striding away.

"Dan has been so nice to Jo," Nell said. "She doesn't know many people here and he's been taking her around and introducing her."

And dancing and laughing with her. Fay thought.

"He really is a good-hearted man," Nell added.

But he's mine, Fay wanted to say. Which wasn't really true. Not when he seemed to prefer the wicked stepsister. She sighed. Unfair. Jo wasn't wicked. What woman could resist being charmed by Dan?

Her father returned, Dan in tow.

"What happened to you?" Dan asked, peering at her ankle.

"I twisted it."

"Ice is the answer," he said. "Give me the keys to your car."

Fay handed over her car keys and he gave them to her dad. "You and Nell can get Fay's car back to her after the reception is over. I'll drive her home in mine."

Her father clapped Dan on the back. "Good idea."

"Say goodbye to Jo for me," Dan told Nell. With that, he scooped Fay up in his arms and carried her from the hall.

His car was near the entrance and he eased her into the front seat. She waited until he got in and started the engine before saying, "Thanks. I'm sorry I interrupted your fun."

He shot her a puzzled look.

"Actually," she went on, "you could have had Jo drive my car and follow you over to my place so she wouldn't get lost. Then you could've taken her back to the reception with you and you wouldn't have had to say goodbye to her."

"What's wrong with my arrangement?"

"Nothing, but—"

He interrupted. "Never mind, I get it. I don't understand why, but this is about Jo, isn't it?"

"I'm not jealous!"

"Whoa. No one accused you of that."

Fay knew she should leave well enough alone, but

she couldn't. "The two of you seemed to be having a good time, that's all."

He didn't answer. They drove in silence while she tried and failed to think of what else to say. Nothing came to mind, probably because she'd said too much already.

Dan used his cell phone to call Clara and alert her, so that she was ready to open the door when she saw the car drive up and Dan lift Fay out. He carried her in and deposited her on the couch.

"My, my, what a shame," Clara said. "Is there anything I can do to help?"

"Ice for Fay's ankle," Dan told her.

"I have just the thing—one of those old-fashioned ice bags. I'll fetch it."

While he waited, he checked on Marie, who was asleep in her crib. "The baby's fine," he told Fay, who nodded in response.

This wasn't how he'd envisioned the post-reception. An injured, unhappy Fay. And unreasonable? As far as he was concerned, yes. What had he done other than dance with Jo? He'd wanted to get to know her a little since she was now Fay's stepsister.

Clara came back with the filled ice bag, wrapped a hand towel around Fay's ankle and applied the bag. "I put coconut drops in the cookie jar," she told them. "And there's coffee waiting."

"You're a dear," Fay said. "Thanks for everything."

"You be sure to give me a ring if you need anything. Promise me you will."

Fay nodded to relieve Clara's mind.

"I'll just run along, then."

Once Clara had gone, Fay said to Dan, "You can run along, too. I'll be fine."

He frowned. "But I'm not a dear. That it?"

Fay bit her lip. "Sorry. I'm grateful you took the trouble to bring me home."

"Grateful but teed off?"

"I hate being clumsy."

He stared down at her. "Who doesn't? Be honest. What's bugging you has nothing to do with clumsiness."

She wouldn't look at him.

"If you're waiting for an apology from me," he said, "you may as well give it up."

That got to her. She glared up at him. "Maybe if you got me some aspirin, I'd feel better."

"Glad to. But if that's meant to make me feel guilty because I'm ignoring your pain, forget it. Pain isn't what the problem is, either." Leaving her with that, Dan went into the bathroom and checked the medicine cabinet over the sink. He removed two pills from the bottle, poured a paper cup of water and came back to the couch.

Fay downed the pills, handed him back the empty cup and sighed. "I'm really mad at myself," she confessed. "Jealousy is an ugly emotion."

"Tell me. I've suffered a few slugs of it myself."

"Over Jean?"

He shook his head. "Over you. Totally unreasonable, but there it is."

Her eyes widened. "But I've never done—" She broke off. "I get the point. You've never done anything, either, not really."

He smiled at her, pulled a chair close to the couch and sat down. "I figured on a wild and passionate reunion, but I'll settle for this." Leaning over, he gave her a sweet and tender kiss.

"That qualifies you for dear," she murmured.

"I'll stay the night in case you need me to fetch the baby or whatever. Like the cabin, except I'll be the one on the couch."

"I wanted the wild and passionate, too," she admitted. "I missed you."

"Yeah, it's no fun hanging out with a cop."

"Oh, come on, we've had lots of fun."

"Tell me you weren't angry when I didn't call you for two weeks."

She sighed. "I thought you'd given up on us."

"We've barely gotten started."

"Yes, but..." Her words trailed off. She'd been about to reveal too much and she didn't want to go that route.

"I think I'm beginning to understand what Jean must have felt." After a beat she added, "Not that I feel the way she did."

He ran the back of his hand along her cheek. "Try to remember I like what I do."

His words lingered in her mind long after he'd settled himself onto the couch, but it was his touch that she carried into her dreams.

Chapter Fourteen

When Fay woke on Sunday morning and tried to stand up, she had to bite back a scream. No way could she walk on her left leg. She hopped to the bathroom on the right leg, then retreated back to bed. Dan fixed her breakfast and served her in bed.

"I called in, hoping I could take some time off," he told her. "No go. We've got a break in the case they need me to follow up on right away. So I called your dad. He and Nell are coming over to help out."

"Thanks. If this blasted ankle didn't hurt so much, I'd let you know exactly how much I appreciate your tender care."

He gave her a lingering kiss, said, "I'll take a rain check," and was gone.

Her father arrived soon after, bringing Jo in to say goodbye.

"My mother's waiting in the car to take me to the

airport to catch my flight back to Chicago,'' Jo said, ''so we don't have time to talk. I do hope we can find that time someday soon. Sorry about your accident.'' She flashed her transforming smile at Fay. ''You know, I never expected to have a stepsister.'' She looked down at the baby sleeping in the cradle. ''What a sweetie. And to think she's my niece. I'm really thrilled about being an aunt. I warn you, I'm planning to spoil her.''

''Every child needs an aunt,'' Fay said. ''Danny Marie is lucky to have you.'' She smiled at Jo. ''Like you, I've never had a sister until now. We'll have to find out what it really means.''

Jo nodded, hugged her and hurried out, leaving Fay regretting her unreasonable jealousy all over again. She liked what she'd seen of Jo and really was looking forward to getting better acquainted.

Nell returned, and with her help and her father's, Fay got through Sunday, but knew she would have to call her client and cancel Monday. And also have her doctor take a look at the ankle.

As she'd suspected, there was no break. ''What you're experiencing is the normal healing process,'' Dr. Morse told her. ''Stay off the ankle as much as possible.''

Fay discussed this and the proposed New York trip with her father and Nell while they drove her back from the doctor's office. Her father was all for her staying off work for the rest of the week, which she refused to do. But, providing her ankle improved by then, they offered to take care of Danny Marie so she could make the New York trip at the end of August.

''It's so lucky we had to delay our honeymoon

cruise until mid-September,'' Nell said. ''How awful if we'd been gone and you had to struggle through this alone.''

''I don't think I ever realized how to appreciate family,'' Fay confessed.

Her dad smiled at her. ''Never too late. And this way we get to see a lot of that grandbaby of mine.''

''Of ours,'' Nell corrected. ''I'm her Nana, you know.''

So Nell was, Fay realized. Danny Marie was lucky to have both a grandmother and grandfather. Her only ones, since neither of Ken's parents were alive.

Fay realized because of Dan's case, chances were he wouldn't be able to come and stay the night, so before her dad left that evening, she had him move the cradle back beside her bed. Nell stacked some diapers and wipes on the dresser so she could tend the baby in the night without having to go as far as the nursery.

Her dad alerted Clara who promised to be on call and to come in and check on Fay in the morning.

Before Fay fell asleep, Dan called her on her cell phone. ''How're you doing?'' he asked.

''Dad and Nell have everything arranged so I can get through the night okay,'' she told him. ''And Clara's ready to pop over if I need anything.''

''I wish I could be with you.''

So did she. ''I'm doing fine,'' she insisted, then told him what the doctor had said. ''In no time at all I'll be as good as new.''

But in the morning when she tried to put weight on her left leg, she realized it might take longer than she thought. She was glad to have Nell and her dad's help. Though she did manage to drive to work on

Wednesday, her ankle was really aching by the time she got home.

Dan came by briefly on Thursday, long enough for a hug and kiss, but couldn't stay. "I'll try to make it Sunday," he told her, "but don't count on it. We're about to wrap up a case."

Somehow she got through Friday and the weekend. Though Nell and her dad came by every day, Dan was tied up all of Sunday. When he arrived just after nine that night, she threw her arms around him, kissing him enthusiastically.

"I do appreciate a warm welcome," he told her as he reluctantly let her go.

"Can you stay?" she asked.

"Would I have let you go if I could?" Maybe they had time for a quickie, but he wanted more with Fay. Needed more.

As they moved into the living room, he watched her limp along, trying not to put too much weight on her leg and said, "Going to take more time than you thought, right?"

She sighed. "Looks that way. But at least the swelling's gone down."

The baby wailed. "She's in the cradle in the bedroom," Fay said as he headed for the nursery. He turned about-face and located the baby.

"Dan's here, everything's right and tight," he told her as he lifted her from the cradle. She stopped crying to stare at him. "You do know me, don't you?" he said. "I guess maybe you like old Dan." Warmed by the thought as well as the welcome weight of the baby in his arms, he smiled as he carried her to Fay.

To his surprise, she said, "You can feed her. She's been on formula for almost a week now and is doing great. I was warming a bottle in the kitchen when you came.''

''No more nursing?''

''The doctor gave me some medicine to make the milk dry up. In a way it's a relief. Nursing gets to be a hazard when the baby gets teeth.''

''Never thought of that.'' He retrieved the bottle from the warmer and sat next to Fay on the couch.

It felt so right to be here, feeding Marie, with Fay beside him that Dan eased back and relaxed, something he hadn't had much time to do lately. ''Don't let me fall asleep,'' he said, ''I can't stay long.''

''I was hoping…'' Her words trailed off.

What he read in her eyes made his groin tighten. ''Me, too. Maybe next week. I've got a rain check to collect, among other things.''

''That rain check and—'' she gestured at her ankle, ''is all because of that second glass of champagne at the reception.''

He raised a quizzical eyebrow.

''It made me sick, so I had to leave you. By the time I came back to the dance floor you weren't around and Oscar asked me to dance.''

''Who's he?''

''Just call him a reincarnated Fred Astaire who kept me hopping to figure out his fancy steps. Then you danced by with Jo and you both were laughing. I forgot to concentrate on my feet and stumbled. Pseudo-Fred kept me from falling, but not from twisting my ankle. You know the rest.''

He chuckled.

''It's not funny,'' she insisted, but he saw she was smiling. After a moment, she added, ''About next week. Tomorrow, I'm flying to New York with my client and his wife. A business trip for us, shopping for her. I won't be back until late Thursday afternoon."

He frowned. "With that ankle?"

"The client's wife gave me a practical present. A cane. It does help."

"Damn the cane. Why the hell did you agree to go when you barely can walk?"

She sat up straight. "I know what I'm doing. I can—oops, look, she's spit the nipple out. Time to burp her."

His beeper went off. "Looks like you'll have to finish up." He handed the baby to Fay and rose. "Have to head out."

"Will I see you on Thursday?"

"I wish I could tell you, but I don't know. You know I'll be here if I can." Turning, he walked to the front door and let himself out.

As he strode to his car, he muttered to himself about stubborn women who thought getting ahead topped every other thing in life. *What the devil am I doing with a woman like that, anyway?* he asked himself.

Because you know damn well there's no one like Fay, the voice in his head told him. *No one even comes close.*

The next day, as Fay limped aboard the jet, she admitted to herself that Dan had a point. Still, it was none of his business what she chose to do. This was an important meeting for her client and he needed her there.

By Thursday afternoon, when her return flight set down at the airport, Fay was exhausted. Her ankle was no worse, but it still pained her when she walked and that, added to the tension at the meeting, had drained her. She was eager to get home, to make sure Danny Marie was all right, then collapse. Luckily she didn't have to work tomorrow because the trip had been her workweek.

Her father picked her up, assured her the baby was thriving, but that he and Nell could use a rest. "Your mother did most of the baby care when you were little," he said, "I never realized how much time and effort it takes to do for a baby. We enjoyed it, but wouldn't want to try it on a daily basis."

"I can't thank you enough." On impulse, she leaned over and kissed her father on the cheek.

He blinked. Was that a tear in his eye? No, she must be imagining things.

At the apartment, as soon as he'd brought in her suitcase, he said to Nell, "Got everything ready to go?"

"I left a casserole in the fridge, so you won't have to make supper," Nell told Fay. "Danny Marie's just fine. She's sleeping. I hate to rush off like this."

"Don't worry, you both have been wonderful." Fay reached out and hugged Nell. "I'm glad the baby has you for her Nana."

"Remember the chain," her father said as they left.

He was as bad as Dan. Which reminded her all over again that she didn't know when she'd see Dan again. Probably not tonight, she figured, since the case was so close to being wrapped up. Which was just as well as she was out on her feet.

He might call though. Then again he might not. Fay limped over and slid on the chain. After she saw that her daughter, now back in the crib, was still sleeping, she settled herself on the couch.

She'd meant it when she'd told Dan she was beginning to understand what Jean had gone through as his wife. It not only must have been the worry that he might be hurt or killed, it also had to be the not knowing when he'd be home and when he wouldn't.

But she didn't intend to let the uncertainty of when she'd see him again affect *her*.

Enough of that. Time to vegetate and watch TV. Fay reached for the remote and clicked it on.

Her father had had it on the local channel, which she ordinarily didn't watch. But the news was on, so she left it there for the moment. A banner flashed across the screen announcing "This just in." It disappeared and the screen showed a chaotic scene of flashing police and ambulance lights. She heard shots fired, though the footage didn't show where they came from or who fired them.

"Heff Gaines, reporting from the intersection of Tenth and Holland," a man said as the news camera zoomed in on him. "We've had a shootout here, at least two men are wounded."

Fay leaned forward, staring at the screen as the camera panned back to the scene, Heff continuing to talk. "To the left a man lies in the street. Another is sprawled on the sidewalk on the other side of that car, impossible to see from this angle."

Peering at the screen, she gasped. No, it couldn't be! But, though it was hard to see, the license on the car Heff spoke of was full of sixes. Dan's car. Hand to her throat, she stared at the body lying face-down, unmoving, in the street.

As Heff continued to describe the scene, sirens

screamed and more police cars pulled up. "I have it on good authority," Heff said, "that one of the men down is a cop."

Fay closed her eyes momentarily, clenching her hands together. Not Dan. It couldn't be Dan.

When she stared at the screen again, she thought she could tell that the man in the street didn't have on a police uniform. Which didn't mean he wasn't a cop—he could be a detective. But not Dan, she refused to believe it was Dan.

"I'm told paramedics have been able to reach the wounded man on the sidewalk," Heff went on. "Police are securing the area to enable them to reach the man in the street. No information on which one is the cop."

Moments later one of the ambulances roared off, lights flashing, siren whooping. "They're taking one of the wounded men to City Hospital," Heff said.

Her gaze never leaving the screen, Fay fumbled for her cell phone and punched in Clara's number.

"I have to go out," Fay told her when she answered, "could you possibly come back over?"

When Clara arrived, Heff was still at the scene. "Someone is heading for the man down in the street," he said.

"Oh, my goodness," Clara exclaimed, "Heff Gaines is the newscaster for the local station. Is this real?"

Fay nodded.

A uniformed policeman, weaving back and forth, was almost to the body. Fay tensed, expecting he'd be shot at. When he reached the victim, he flung down a blanket, rolled the inert man onto it and folded the blanket over him. Pulling the blanket with him, he reached relative safety behind the car. Dan's car. She could see an ambulance parked farther along the street.

"I'm afraid Dan's been hurt," she told Clara. "I'm going to City Hospital to find out."

"Oh, dear, I do hope he's all right," Clara said.

As Fay grabbed her bag and started for the door, Clara added, "Don't you think you should put on some shoes first?"

Fay hobbled back, slid her feet into her sandals and started off again.

She parked her car as close as she could get to the E.R. entrance of City Hospital and limped past an ambulance with its rear doors wide open. Once inside the waiting room, she found no one was behind the receptionist's window. What now? Push open the inner door and go into the patient area?

"They just wheeled some guy in," a man sitting in one of the waiting room chairs volunteered. "I heard a medic say he got shot."

A uniformed cop burst into the waiting room from the parking lot, glanced around, then hurried through the inner doors. Fay trailed him, limping as fast as she could. The first alcove he passed had a curtain drawn across. The cop slid the curtain partway open, muttered an apology, jerked the curtain into place and strode on.

A nurse in green scrubs coming toward them let him go past, but blocked Fay's passage with a no-nonsense "May I help you?"

"Can you tell me the name of the man just brought in?" Fay asked. "He'd been shot."

"I'm sorry. Information like that is confidential."

"But he may be—that is, I know him and I'm afraid he—"

"Please return to the waiting room. The receptionist will help you if he can."

"He isn't there!" Fay blurted.

"He will be. This way, please." Herding Fay ahead of her, the nurse gave her no choice but to retreat.

"Get anywhere?" the guy in the waiting room asked when she returned.

She shook her head.

"Yeah, most times they won't tell you nothing."

Catching a glimpse of a man in green through the receptionist's window, Fay limped over. "I need to know the name of the man the ambulance just brought in," Fay said. "He was shot."

The man—his name tag said he was George Cox—looked up from the paperwork spread on the desk. "Are you a relative?"

"How do I know if you won't give me his name?" Fay cried.

"If you're not a relative, I can't give you any information."

Fay stared at him in disbelief. Finally she decided to lie. "If his name is Dan Sorenson, then, yes, I'm his sister."

George shuffled through some of the papers, then shook his head. "We haven't treated anyone by that name since I came on duty at three." He cocked his head as though listening and Fay heard the wail of a siren rapidly coming closer.

George turned and called to someone invisible to Fay, "That red blanket's coming in."

Whatever that meant, it could be the other shooting victim. It could be Dan. The paramedics wouldn't be bringing him in through the waiting room, they would wheel the gurney through the outside double doors next to the one she'd come in through. They wouldn't be any more likely than the E.R. personnel to tell her his name, but if she waited out there and could catch a glimpse of who they wheeled past her, then she'd know if it was Dan.

She ducked through the outside door of the waiting room just as the ambulance turned into the E.R. entrance, its siren shutting off abruptly. Limping to the other side of the double doors, she tried to blend herself into the wall, an impossible task since it wasn't yet dusk. They were bound to notice her. The most she could hope for was that they wouldn't bother to make her leave.

A police car, lights flashing, tires squealing, turned into the entrance and came to a stop alongside the ambulance. Two uniformed cops jumped out and strode toward her.

"Ms.," one said, "Get out of the way. Now."

"But I need to know who—" she began.

Her words were cut off abruptly when one of the cops grasped her arm and speed-marched her through the door into the waiting room. He let her go and ordered, "Stay here."

"Please," she called after him as he exited through the inner door of the waiting room. "I need to know—" She stopped when the door closed behind him.

"You don't get nowhere with cops, lady," the guy in the chair said. "Don't waste your breath."

Glancing at the receptionist window, she saw that George was nowhere in sight. Making her way to the inner door, she eased it open a crack and peered through. A paramedic was just pushing a gurney through the double doors. She still had a chance. She muttered a word she rarely said under her breath when the cops behind the paramedic moved up to flank the gurney as it rolled down the hall. The one nearer her completely blocked her view of the occupant's face.

Pushing through the door and running after the gurney would be futile, she knew, so, temporarily frustrated, she was about to close the inner door when a man pushed through the double doors and strode along the hall. She stared at him, her heart hammering.

Throwing open the door, she cried, "Dan!" and flung herself at him.

He caught her, holding her close for a moment, then releasing her, but keeping his hands on her shoulders. "What are you doing here?"

"I saw it on TV and they said a cop got shot and your car was there and I thought—oh, Dan, I thought it was you." She knew she was babbling, but couldn't control herself. "I came to find out, to see you, only they wouldn't—"

"Calm down, Fay. Here I am, unhurt."

"Your car—I saw the license number on TV and I—"

"I was at the scene, yes. Now you need to go home and relax. I'm okay, but I'm still on duty so I can't come with you."

"But you—"

"I'll come when I can. Please go home, Fay."

"If you'll promise you'll come by when you finish up whatever it is you have to do."

"It's likely to be well after midnight."

"I don't care, promise me."

He nodded, let go of her shoulders and continued on down the hall. Fay took a deep breath, let it out with a sigh and limped slowly out of the building and made her way to her car.

Dan was alive, she kept telling herself as she drove home. Alive and not even injured, thank God. By the time she reached the apartment, she was shivering, warm as the August evening was.

Inside, she assured Clara that Dan hadn't been hurt, thanking her for coming to the rescue.

"I'm glad he's all right," Clara said, "but I can see you're still distraught, dear. You need to take a nice warm bath to relax you."

"I'll do that."

Once Clara was gone, hugging herself to stop the shivers, Fay checked on Danny Marie. Since the baby seemed to be sleeping soundly, she then filled the bath tub. When she lowered herself into the warm water her shaking eased, and, after a few minutes of soaking, her tenseness began to ebb.

The name of Dan's ex-wife popped into her head. Jean had given him up rather than go through the worry of wondering if she'd ever see him alive again. She'd thought she understood Jean's point of view, but now she knew she really hadn't. Being a cop's wife *was* a difficult proposition. No wonder he'd made up his mind never to marry again.

On the other hand, a cop's life was a difficult proposition. Didn't he deserve someone to be there when he needed her? Someone strong enough to survive the times she wasn't sure he'd come home alive. Jean hadn't been that woman, but did that mean there was no woman who wouldn't feel being married to Dan was worth the worry and uncertainty?

By the time she climbed out of the tub, Fay was completely relaxed. And exhausted. She donned a robe, stretched out on her bed and fell asleep. The baby's wails roused her. She sat up, groggy, and peered at the clock's red numbers. Almost three. A new morning.

Later, sitting in the nursery rocking chair feeding Danny Marie, she told her daughter, "Some babies sleep through the night by your age. It'd be nice if you'd think about doing the same."

After being burped, Danny Marie showed no sign of being sleepy. Fay yawned and resigned herself to amusing the baby for a while. She enjoyed playing with her daughter, but preferably during daylight hours.

"I think you're spoiled," she murmured. "Everyone caters to you. Me, Clara, my dad and Nell, even Dan when he's here."

Danny Marie smiled at her and Fay buried her face in the baby's neck, smelling the indefinably wonderful scent of baby.

After rearranging the baby on her lap, she said, "Maybe your mommy won't work so many days a week once this job she's on is finished. What do you think of that? And maybe once Mommy's relationship with Dan settles down, you'll see more of him, too. I know you like him. I do, too. He'd make a great father, wouldn't he?"

Fay paused, her last few words echoing in her mind. How could Dan ever be Danny Marie's father when he didn't want to marry? Well, of course she didn't either, did she? She'd told herself she'd never marry after breaking her engagement to Ken. Then, somehow, his dying had etched her negative view of marriage into stone.

Fay blinked. Could guilt have had anything to do with her decision? After a moment she shook her head. No, she had perfectly rational reasons for staying single and she could name them one by one.

A line from some great writer—Shakespeare?—popped unbidden into her head. "Methinks the lady doth protest too much."

Chapter Fifteen

Dan checked his watch when he left the hospital. After three. Should he stop by Fay's at this hour of the morning? He'd promised her, though. Besides, tired as he was, he needed to go home to Fay.

Home to Fay? No, that wasn't right, why had he thought that? What he meant was he needed to be with her, if only for a few minutes. But a part of his mind wouldn't let go of the connection between home and Fay.

As he pulled out of the parking lot, he relived the way she'd thrown her arms around him in the E.R. She cared about him, that was obvious. But, by now, she'd have settled down and had time to think about the anguish she'd undoubtedly gone through. Would she greet him with open arms or tell him goodbye, having persuaded herself she didn't want to go through that again?

He wouldn't blame her, but he hoped to hell she still wanted to keep seeing him. He sighed, wondering if he'd ever get over her.

It looked like his partner Gary was going to make it, thank God. Best cop on his team. If the bullet had caught him an inch higher he'd have bought the farm. Wasn't his time to go, obviously.

When Dan turned onto Fay's street he saw she'd left her porch light on, so she must be expecting him. But that didn't necessarily mean she'd welcome him. Reaction was settling in. By the time he got out of the car, the adrenaline high of the confrontation at Tenth and Holland and its aftermath was pretty much depleted.

He rang Fay's doorbell, giving his name when she asked who was there. She opened the door, peered at him through the crack left by the chain, then closed the door so she could unhook the chain and let him in.

As he entered, he saw she was in her robe, hair tousled as though she'd been sleeping—just the way he liked her best. In her arms, Marie stared up at him. He'd no sooner kicked the door shut with his foot and put the chain back on, than Fay thrust the baby at him.

"I've had hours to think about it," Fay announced, "and I've decided that Danny Marie needs her father."

Startled, he asked, "Danny Marie?"

"Her real name is Danielle Marie. I didn't tell you before because I wasn't sure you'd be pleased."

He looked from her to the baby and back, feeling dangerously near tears. "You named her after me?"

"Who else? If it hadn't been for you, neither the

baby nor I would be alive. She owes you her life and so do I. You know what the Chinese say about saving a person's life, don't you?''

Where was this going? ''Something about the saver being responsible for the person he saved for the rest of that person's life, as I recall.''

She nodded. ''Since you saved Danny Marie and me as a package deal, you're stuck with both of us. For once my father was right about me never doing any better.''

He tried to make sense of what she was saying. ''If you mean me, your dad's words were more like you could do worse.''

She waved a hand. ''Whatever. The truth is, Danny Marie and I both need you. You're her father already, in most ways that count. As for me—'' She broke off and sighed. ''I got scared out of my wits when I saw your car in the middle of that shoot-out or whatever it was. But I'm not Jean. I can live with it because otherwise I'd really have to live without you. So get rid of the notion I don't want to live with a detective. I—I—'' Again she faltered. She swallowed, lifted the baby from his arms and headed for the nursery.

Dan trailed her, still trying to figure out what she was leading up to. Standing on the opposite side, he watched her lay his namesake in the crib. For a moment both of them stood looking down at the now drowsy baby.

''You what?'' Dan asked after a minute.

''If you must know, I love you so much, no other man will ever do.'' Her words came out defiantly, almost angrily. ''It can only be you. Now and always. So, will you marry me?''

He couldn't believe his ears. He'd about decided

she might be going to propose they live together—but marry her?

"Well?" she demanded. "Did you leave your tongue home with your cat?"

Speechless didn't halfway describe his condition. Dumbfounded, aghast, shocked, knocked for a loop, and plain old flabbergasted were all crowded together.

"I didn't expect—" he began.

"I don't care what you expected." She kept her voice low to avoid disturbing the baby, but urgency throbbed through each word. "Answer me."

"Man, what a boss you'd make," he said, skirting the crib and taking her arm to lead her from the nursery into the living room.

"Don't change the subject!"

"All I was trying to say is you sure make it tough on a poor plodding detective who isn't used to you high-powered types."

"Don't make fun of me. This is my life. And yours."

He put his palm to her cheek, looking into her changeable eyes. "I'm not making fun. I figure I began to love you the moment I hauled you off the porch of my cabin, half-dead and pregnant. And it's gotten worse since. Speaking about our lives, you've got to realize it scares the hell out of me to tell you I love you, because, to me, that's a life-long commitment. The kind you get married for."

"Too scared to come right out with it?"

"Woman, you don't know what you're asking for."

"Oh, yes, I do. And I still haven't gotten a definitive answer."

He leaned so close to her their breath mingled.

"Here goes. Listen up. I love you. I want you for my wife. Forever."

Tears filled her eyes. "Oh, Dan," she whispered. "That was so romantic."

It was? His surprise at her words didn't prevent him from kissing her, though he pulled away after a moment to murmur, "Those better be tears of happiness."

Then he put his heart into the kiss, holding her hard against him. He wasn't quite sure how she'd forced his hand, made him face what was happening to him. Marriage might scare him, but he knew now he was ready and willing to do anything to make Fay his.

"Do you know you smell of roses, but you're the spiciest gal I've ever met," he told her as, between kisses, they made their way to her bedroom.

"Do you know you're the sexiest man I've ever met?" she countered.

He grinned at her. "Why else would you ask me to marry you?"

"Try because I figured it'd be forever before you asked me. Someone had to put the kettle on the fire or it'd never boil."

"Lady, there's a lot more than a kettle boiling right now."

By the time he'd shed his clothes and she'd removed her robe, and they were in bed together, his need for her was overwhelming. But he took time to explore her breasts, something he hadn't had the chance to do much of before she stopped nursing, touching them, tasting them, teasing her nipples erect until she moaned.

"I hear there's all sorts of tasty things to do with whipped cream and chocolate syrup," he murmured.

"Heavens, the company you keep." Her husky whisper told him how much she wanted him. "I'll stock up."

Then she claimed his mouth, deepening the kiss, her hands caressing him, her fingers seeking out places on his body he hadn't even known were touch-sensitive. Not interrupting the kiss, he slid over her until his arousal was nestled between her thighs.

She opened to him, an invitation he couldn't resist. Plunged deep into her warmth, he had a fleeting memory about once vowing to bring her to the point where she wouldn't know where she left off and he began. Hell, here he'd gone and done it to himself. They were one, he and Fay, and, at the moment, nothing else existed.

Afterward, he fell asleep with her in his arms.

He woke to daylight and found Fay next to him, up on one elbow, her gaze fixed on his face.

"Trying to decide if I'm worth it?" he murmured.

"Just admiring the first man I've ever slept all night with. Which will end in a minute because your namesake is beginning to stir. Shall we toss to see who gets up and feeds her?"

Before he could answer, she said, "No, wait, I have a better idea. I'll feed her here in bed while you tell me what happened on Tenth and Holland. Or as much of it as you can share." She gave him a quick kiss and rose.

He took a bathroom break, returned to bed and closed his eyes, lying there with what he knew must be a sappy smile on his face. What a package deal, Fay and Peanut both his.

In a few minutes Fay was back with the baby and a bottle. She propped herself up so she could hold

Danny Marie comfortably and began to feed her. "So, got your story straight?" she asked.

He told her what wasn't classified about the shoot-out, finishing up with, "Gary Livinsky was the only one who got a straight shot at the perp. Nailed him. But it gave away Gary's location to the other perp, who shot him. That guy got away. Not for long, though. Before I left the hospital, I heard he'd been captured. It was touch and go with Gary for a few hours. I stayed around until I knew he'd pull through."

"How about the guy he shot?"

"He'll live, worse luck, and be around to cost the taxpayers more money."

"I'm glad your friend Gary will be okay."

"So are his wife and two kids."

She raised an eyebrow. "I thought you told me cop marriages always failed."

"Lots do."

"But not all. Ours won't. I'm in for the long haul."

He grinned at her. His Ms. Know-It-All.

"Do you think your brother will be upset about us getting married?" she asked.

That came out of the blue, as far as he was concerned. "You mean Bruce? Why should he?"

"I got the impression he didn't want me to stay in the cabin with you."

Dan chuckled. "Maybe so, but it had nothing to do with you. He was worried I wouldn't understand that a woman who's recently delivered a baby is off bounds sexually. You don't want to hear the lesson he read me."

Fay finished feeding Danny Marie, burped her and laid the baby between them.

"Hi, kid," Dan said. "Think you'll like your new dad?"

His namesake turned her head and regarded him solemnly for a long moment before smiling. He leaned over and kissed the top of her head.

"You know," he told Fay, "it might have taken me a while to admit to myself how I felt about you, but, from the moment I first held her, in my heart Peanut—Danny Marie—has always been mine."

Four months later, just before Christmas, Fay's father led her down the aisle of St. Dunstan's, the same church he'd married Nell in. Seeing Dan at the altar, waiting for her, Fay remembered her momentary vision of the two of them at this altar and smiled. She hadn't realized then marriage to Dan was what she wanted, but sometimes even unrecognized dreams come true.

All the Sorensons had come for the wedding, including Will, the brother she hadn't met before. And Dan's father, up from Florida. But not, of course, Dan's mother. Which might have made her sad if this hadn't been such a joyous occasion that nothing could get her down.

Fay viewed the ceremony through a happy blur, not quite believing it was real. Once they were really and truly married, sealed with a kiss, and she'd hurried from the church with Dan, only then did it have any reality to her.

"You didn't seem too uneasy," she told Dan as the limo drove them to their reception.

"That's 'cause I was in a fog. Didn't even manage to tell you how beautiful you look."

"Should I believe a man who told me he thought I was beautiful even in the cabin, anemia and all?"

"You were and you are."

"Did I ever tell you I foresaw us getting married when we were at Dad and Nell's wedding? It shook me up so much I had to drink those two flutes of champagne to recover."

"Still jealous of your stepsister?"

She smiled. "As long as you remember which sister you're supposed to take on the honeymoon, you can dance with Jo all you want."

He pulled her closer and kissed her all the rest of the way to the reception hall.

"Out!" Fourteen-month-old Danny Marie demanded, using one of the words in her increasing vocabulary. She reached for the doorknob of the cabin, fortunately not quite within her grasp.

"Hang in there, kid," Dan told her. "It might be summer everywhere else, but even though it's almost July, the U.P. doesn't always realize that. You need your jacket on."

He was amazed and pleased at how enthusiastically his daughter had taken to the woods. When he'd suggested to Fay that they spend his June vacation in the cabin, he'd known she'd like the idea, but Marie was a question.

They'd solved the problem of Spot by bringing the cat with them and dropping him off with Megan. No way was he going to leave any animal in a boarding cage for a month.

Fay slipped a jacket on Danny Marie, then one on herself, and the three of them ventured out into the sunny but cool afternoon. The toddler immediately spotted a chipmunk and ran ahead, trying to catch it. The chipmunk disappeared into a fallen log and she stopped and peered into the log.

When her parents caught up, she said, "Gone."

"That's a chipmunk for you," Dan said. "Now you see him, now you don't."

"When you were a little baby," Fay told her, "your father and I used to take you for walks in this woods. Daddy carried you in a little pouch."

"Daddy carry," she repeated and Dan swung her up into his arms. Almost immediately she wanted down and wandered happily between the trees.

Never in his wildest dreams had he ever pictured the three of them together over a year later in this same woods. A real family.

Later, back in the cabin, a sleepy Danny Marie didn't want to lie on the couch for her nap. Dan picked her up, brought her to the old bentwood rocker that Megan had insisted they needed in the cabin, and sat down with her in his lap.

"Bye, baby," she insisted.

"Bye baby bunting," he sang. "Daddy's gone a-hunting..." As he repeated the familiar words, he had the satisfaction of knowing that's exactly what he was—her daddy.

She fell asleep and he carried her to the couch. "Double solitaire?" he asked Fay.

She shook her head. "Scrabble, maybe."

"Or we could just fool around."

"That's the best offer I've ever had in this cabin," she told him.

In the loft, she fell into his arms and they took a slow, sweet ride to completion.

Afterward he said, "Some would say fate led you to this cabin and into my arms."

She'd been putting off telling him, but here was the perfect opening. "Speaking of fate," she began. "Well, not exactly fate because how was I to know I'd tucked away an outdated prescription in a dresser drawer? I do tend to save things, then forget how old they are."

"So?"

"You remember how I ran out and had to have Dr. Morse call in a new prescription?"

He shook her head.

"Well, I did and he did," she went on. "Right after I called him, I found this other packet in the dresser and began taking those first. I did pick up the new ones, but went on with the others I found in the dresser until the container was empty. When I went to throw it away, I happened to see how outdated it was. Two years! I couldn't believe I'd done something that—well, foolish."

"What pills are you talking about?"

"My birth control pills."

He rose up onto one elbow and stared down at her. "Don't tell me this is a roundabout way of letting me know you're pregnant."

She bit her lip. "I knew you'd be annoyed, but I really didn't do it on purpose. At least I don't think so. I mean, it affects me, too. I'll have to cut back still more on my work."

Dan took a deep breath and whooshed it out. "Do I have this straight? Danny Marie's not going to be an only child?"

"Actually, once we got married, I really didn't

want her to be. But, believe me, I never would have gone behind your back to—to—'' her voice quivered.

He pulled her into his arms.

''You're not angry?'' she asked.

He held her closer, his lips nuzzling her neck.

Angry, no. Some scared, yes. Bringing a child into today's world worried him. But Danny Marie had taught him some things were worth the worry.

Into her ear, he said, ''A twist of fate brought you to me. Why should I get upset because another of fate's tricks is making me a father for the second time? No, sweetheart, I'm happy for us.''

He held her a little away from him and smiled. ''But please, let's arrange it so I don't have to deliver this new one.''

* * * * *

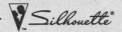

SPECIAL EDITION™

Separated at birth, triplets Lissa, Adam and Sam were unaware of each other's existence until circumstances brought them together.

Because birthright has its privileges and family ties run deep.

THE VIRGIN'S MAKEOVER
by Judy Duarte
(Silhouette Special Edition #1593, available February 2004)

TAKE A CHANCE ON ME
by Karen Rose Smith
(Silhouette Special Edition #1599, available March 2004)

AND THEN THERE WERE THREE
by Lynda Sandoval
(Silhouette Special Edition #1605, available April 2004)

Available at your favorite retail outlet.

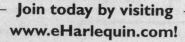
INTCOMM

If you enjoyed what you just read,
then we've got an offer you can't resist!

Take 2 bestselling love stories FREE!
Plus get a FREE surprise gift!

Clip this page and mail it to Silhouette Reader Service™

IN U.S.A.
3010 Walden Ave.
P.O. Box 1867
Buffalo, N.Y. 14240-1867

IN CANADA
P.O. Box 609
Fort Erie, Ontario
L2A 5X3

YES! Please send me 2 free Silhouette Special Edition® novels and my free surprise gift. After receiving them, if I don't wish to receive anymore, I can return the shipping statement marked cancel. If I don't cancel, I will receive 6 brand-new novels every month, before they're available in stores! In the U.S.A., bill me at the bargain price of $3.99 plus 25¢ shipping and handling per book and applicable sales tax, if any*. In Canada, bill me at the bargain price of $4.74 plus 25¢ shipping and handling per book and applicable taxes**. That's the complete price and a savings of at least 10% off the cover prices—what a great deal! I understand that accepting the 2 free books and gift places me under no obligation ever to buy any books. I can always return a shipment and cancel at any time. Even if I never buy another book from Silhouette, the 2 free books and gift are mine to keep forever.

235 SDN DNUR
335 SDN DNUS

Name	(PLEASE PRINT)	
Address	Apt.#	
City	State/Prov.	Zip/Postal Code

* Terms and prices subject to change without notice. Sales tax applicable in N.Y.
** Canadian residents will be charged applicable provincial taxes and GST.
   All orders subject to approval. Offer limited to one per household and not valid to current Silhouette Special Edition® subscribers.
   ® are registered trademarks of Harlequin Books S.A., used under license.

SPED02   ©1998 Harlequin Enterprises Limited

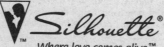

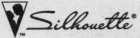

COMING NEXT MONTH

#1603 PRICELESS—Sherryl Woods
Million Dollar Destinies
Famed playboy Mack Carlton loved living the fast life—with even faster women—until he met Dr. Beth Browning. Beth's reserved, quiet ways brought out the deepest emotions in Mack, and soon had him wanting to believe in a slow and easy, forever kind of love. Could Mack convince Beth that his bachelor days were over?

#1604 FOREVER...AGAIN—Maureen Child
Merlyn County Midwives
You don't get a second chance at forever. That's what widower Ron Bingham believed. But, then, he hadn't counted on meeting PR whiz Lily Cunningham. The carefree beauty brought laughter and passion back into his life and made him wonder—was love even sweeter the second time around?

#1605 CATTLEMAN'S HEART—Lois Faye Dyer
Chaotic. That was the only way Rebecca Wallingford could describe her latest business trip. The superorganized accountant had been sent to oversee the expansion of a certain Jackson Rand's ranch. She'd never meant to get pulled into a whirlwind love affair with the rugged rancher...and she certainly hadn't planned on liking it!

#1606 THE SHEIK & THE PRINCESS IN WAITING—
Susan Mallery
Prince Reyhan had been commanded by his father, the King of Bahania, to marry as befit his position. There was just one tiny matter in the way: divorcing his estranged wife, Emma Kennedy. Seeing sweet Emma again brought back a powerful attraction...and something deeper. Could Reyhan choose duty over his heart's desire?

#1607 THE BEST OF BOTH WORLDS—Elissa Ambrose
Single. Unemployed. Pregnant. Becky Roth had a lot on her mind...not to mention having to break her pregnancy news to the father, Carter Prescott III. They'd shared one amazing night of passion. But small-town, small-*time* Becky was no match for Carter's blue-blooded background. The fact that she was in love with him didn't change a thing.

#1608 IN HER HUSBAND'S IMAGE—Vivienne Wallington
Someone was trying to sabotage Rachel Hammond's ranch. The widowed single mom's brother-in-law, Zack Hammond, arrived and offered to help find the culprit...but the sexy, rugged photographer stirred up unwelcome memories of their scandalous past encounter. Now it was just a matter of time before a shattering secret was revealed!

SSECNM0304R

SPECIAL EDITION